Jane Og

Psychology at th
where she te
nutrition, dieteti
five academic books: Fat Chance: the Myth of
Dieting (1992; Routledge), Health Psychology: a
textbook (4th edition, 2007; Open University
Press); Health and the construction of the
individual. (2002; Routledge); The psychology of
eating: From healthy to disordered behaviour (2nd
edition 2009: Blackwell); Essential readings in
health psychology (2007; Open University Press)
and has published over 100 journal articles on
aspects of psychology particularly eating
behaviour and obesity, aspects of women's health
and the role of language. She has also written
many articles for more popular magazines and
newspapers and is a regular featured expert on the
TV, radio and for women's magazines. This is her
first novel and was written after a family holiday in
Cuba. It is the manifestation of a clichéd mid life
career crisis and the desire to see if she could write
fiction after all these years of writing fact. Jane is
44 and lives with her husband and two children in
Guildford.

Jane Ogden

Chasing the Cuba Libre

Chasing the Cuba Libre

First published by Lulu Press 2011

Cover based on a painting by Jane Ogden

ISBN 978-1-4467-4810-7

To David, Harry and Ellie.

One

Jackie sat in the taxi on the way home feeling woozy. It had been her last night out with friends before they headed off for their family holidays and they had spent the evening drinking wine and contemplating full-on family life for the next few weeks. At her front door she fumbled for her key and let herself in. Her lodger, Carl, was still out, but Andrew had left the landing light on and as she made her way up the stairs she could see that he was reading in bed. He looked up as she got undressed, saying 'I've kept your side warm' and they turned the lights off as she got under the duvet. She lay there in the dark deciding whether she should snuggle up to him or not. Then she noticed that she was having to decide and thought how sad that was. The spontaneity of it all had gone, and even the smallest signs of affection now needed to be planned.

She felt Andrew's hand touch her shoulder then travel down her back as he guided her towards him. She let him put his arm around her and she laid her head on his chest. Years ago she would have succumbed to him, wrapped herself around him, nustled into him. Now her body felt hard and they no longer seemed to fit well together. Her knees were facing away as if trying to escape and her hand felt rigid and couldn't find a good position on his back. And she knew she was watching herself as he gently stroked her hair. Then, as he turned her face up to his and kissed her, she flinched but resisted the urge to pull away. They used to love kissing. She used to say 'never let us stop kissing'. Now it felt forced. It was wet, his tongue felt intrusive in her mouth and he had a taste and a smell that wasn't right. She coughed to move her head away. 'A marriage isn't a marriage without sex' she thought. But what used to feel sexy and passionate now felt fumbling and irritating. She felt annoyed by his pacing. Too slow or too fast but never right. Always out of sync with her, no longer able to read her signals with no idea that she was miles behind him. He was doing what he had learned to do to her 14 years ago. Then it had worked. She'd thought he was great in bed. Now his touch felt in the wrong place at the wrong time. And just when she manoeuvred him to make it work, he would stop and move on to somewhere else. Then she noticed her hands, still firmly fixed on his back. She hadn't touched him at all, no interest in exploring, no curiosity about his body, no desire to turn him on. She was rigid, stuck and she watched herself being so.

But time is a strange force in sex and gradually the biology of her body was allowed to take over. The voices in her head went quiet and her mind was still. Years of experience had taught her the right positions for her and she enabled herself to become involved.

'That was nice' Andrew said when they had finished. 'We should do it more often.'

'Yes. It was lovely' Jackie said as she rolled over. 'I'm tired. I need to get to sleep.'

She found the edge of the bed, pulled her knees up and hugged herself. 'I need to make my marriage work' she thought. But she felt hollow, empty, detached and she lay there in the dark as the tears slowly and silently slid down her face. 'How did I get here? How on earth did I get here?'

It'd been fourteen years. They had a nice house, lovely family, good jobs and lots in common. They could talk about work, friends, the state of the world and ideas. And they lived together well. He shopped, she did the washing. He cooked, she cleaned. He did the money, she did the kids. They were a good unit. They functioned. They worked. They even like the same holidays and planned adventures to interesting places. Many a struggling couple would have loved to have had what they had. They sat in their marriage counselling being articulate and talking to each other and their counsellor thought they were fine. 'You still respect each other' she said. 'You have so much going for you'. But Jackie wanted more.

She felt numb, cold, shut down and trapped. When he laughed, she didn't see what was funny. When he was sad, she was irritated. When she made him upset, she could see what she had done but felt no guilt, no remorse. She flinched when he touched her and she avoided his eyes. She wanted to feel right, to know that she could still feel and to know that she hadn't died inside. And she wanted moments. Moments that she seemed to have with everyone else. Moments that give life its lifts and make all the rest of the slog seem worth it.

The following day was her last at work before their big trip, and she went straight home to find Andrew cooking dinner and her children watching a film.

'Why do you always let them watch so much TV?' she snapped. 'They have so many books to read and toys to play with. It's just lazy parenting.'

'Hello, Jackie' replied Andrew. 'Did you have a nice day?'

Dinner was soon ready and they sat down at the table. Jackie always tried to eat with the kids and had instigated a family ritual whereby they each had to say three things about their day. This was an attempt to get around her children's tendency to say 'nothing', 'the usual' or 'can't remember' whenever asked about school and over the years the ritual had become entrenched. Now they prepared to take their turn. It was Toby's time to start.

'We are learning about the Romans and today we looked at pictures of Hadrian's Wall and had to think why they needed to build such a long wall and why their roads are so straight. We had PE and I did tennis and then we had art and I drew a picture of a dragon'.

'That sounds like a nice day darling' said Jackie. 'Do you remember when we went along the Roman road up north that time?

Do you know why it was so straight?'

'It was because the Romans could just build through anything that was in their way,' said Andrew.

'We know that you know,' said Jackie raising her eyes to the ceiling in the way that she had learned so well from her mother's reaction to her father.

Next, Vicky described her three things. Then it was Andrew's turn. When Jackie had met Andrew she thought him the most interesting man she had ever met. He, in turn, had been quite reticent to talk about his work, his extensive knowledge about everything or his slightly wacky ideas, and it had been Jackie's role to bring him out of himself, which she had done with great pleasure. He had lived the life of the intellectual recluse and she had found that, with the right questions, a good basic understanding of what he was talking about and a steady use of humour she could get him to open up. This had led to many overly long lunches filled with discussions and explanations of anything Jackie wanted to know. 'Tell me about the history of Pakistan,' she would say and he would. 'Explain theories of reality,' and off he would go. But now, 14 years later, the novelty and her interest had begun to wear thin. Andrew had still maintained the habit of opening up, but she now found her mind drifting on to other areas or watching the clock. Today was no exception, and without realising it, she got up to clear the plates away whilst he was mid flow.

'Jackie, I haven't finished my three things' he said, trying to make a joke of it.

'Oh sorry! I can still hear you from the kitchen'.

'But that's not the point. The kids get their turn. I want mine as well'. It was beginning to sound less of a joke.

Toby and Vicky took their cue from their mum and got down from the table to go into the front room. Jackie sat herself back down at the table and reluctantly asked Andrew to 'go on then'.

He looked up at her wearily and paused.

'Jackie' he said 'We need to talk'

Jackie looked up at him and poured herself a drink.

'You know, I was looking at that photo of you on my desk today - the one with you smiling - and I thought to myself, 'I never see Jackie like that anymore. Not really'. You light up when the kids are around but when it's just us... You are so cold, cool, distant, fed up. I don't recognise you anymore. And you snap. You're rude to me. You never touch me. I try to be around, to be helpful, do whatever I can, but you just don't seem to like me anymore.'

'Andrew. Let's not talk about this now. The kids can hear. They are only next door' she said.

'But the way you speak to me. The way you treat me. It's as if I'm nothing. I put up with it and put with it, hoping it will get better, but it never does'. His voice was getting louder.

'Andrew. Wait 'til the kids are in bed. Please. Not now.'

'You used to care about me. Value me. I see you with your friends being nice, interested, supportive, smiling. I get nothing. Why can't you just treat me like you treat them? It's rubbish, Jackie, it really is'

Jackie could hear the children stirring in the other room.

'Andrew. Shut up. Please shut up. They don't need to be involved'.

'It's horrible to live with it day in, day out'.

'Andrew. Please not now. Stop it.' Her voice was getting louder.

'It's so unfair'

Steps were coming into the room.

'Andrew. Shut up'.

Toby walked in.

'Mummy! You shouted at Daddy. That's rude and horrible. You tell us not to say it and now you are saying it. It's mean.'

Andrew was now sat quietly with tears slowly sliding down his face.

'And you've made Daddy cry' said Toby rushing over to give Andrew a hug. Vicky now came through as well and went straight over to look after her father.

'We heard you arguing Mummy' said Vicky. We heard you telling Daddy to shut up. Why were you so rude to him?'

'Darlings it's complicated. I'm sorry I should never have said it. But these things are difficult. It is just between Daddy and me. I never wanted you two to get involved'

She moved across to hold her children but they clung on tightly to their father who by now was crying and holding them tightly back.

'Adults do have arguments sometimes. Sometimes they shout and say things they shouldn't. It's not all my fault darlings' she said.

'Well it seems like it is' said Toby.

Jackie felt panic rise up through her body. Although her kids clearly loved their father she had always been their favourite. She had been there every day to hug them, talk to them, cook their food, pick them up from school, and know about the ins and outs of their lives. She had played games with them for hours on end and prided herself in being able to develop an interest in whatever was their most recent obsession. Now she felt like she was losing them. It felt unjust. Primeval.

'Andrew, tell them I'm sorry I said it. Andrew, tell them it was both of us not just me'.

Andrew paused and said: 'Mummies and Daddies sometimes argue. Mummy shouldn't have shouted but she was cross'.

A few minutes later, Andrew decided to go out for a walk and Jackie was left to make it up to the kids. They had a bath, got their pyjamas on and settled onto the sofa for their usual story before bed. She had one arm around each of them, and as the story progressed she could feel them starting to relax into her, and by bedtime she knew that she had regained lost ground. Toby had his head snuggled into her shoulder and was holding her hand and Vicky had absent-mindedly placed her leg across hers and was playing with her hair. She clung on to them more tightly than usual and went along with their requests for 'one more chapter' and 'just another, please' and when she kissed them goodnight she told them even more times than usual that she loved them and how special they were.

Andrew came back about an hour later and looked at her, waiting. She paused. It could go either way: anger or apology. And then she realised she didn't feel angry at him anymore. For the first time in years, she felt sorry for him.

'You're right Andrew. Everything you've said is right. I know. I know what I'm like with you. I don't like it. I don't like myself when I'm with you. It's a horrible version of me. You're a good man and you deserve more'.

'And I've been thinking as well, Jackie' he said. 'I'm not coming to Cuba with you. I can't bear it. You've no idea how awful it is being with someone who makes you feel like this. Last year on holiday was dreadful. I'm not going through that again'.

'But it's Cuba, Andrew. I've always wanted to go. The music, the architecture, the politics. It's been my dream. And now the kids are old enough. It will be great'.

'No. I'm not going. I've decided. You go if you want. Take the kids. I'll stay at home'

'Do you mean this Andrew, or are you just angry?' she asked.

'I mean it'

'Like you meant it when you threatened not to go away last year or the year before?'

'No. I mean it. I'm not going'.

Jackie spent the night lying in bed trying to work things out. She so wanted to go. Cuba had always been her fantasy. Che Guevara, the revolution and the passion of the heat and the music. She'd always been a good socialist at heart and the idea of a small group of rebels beating the ruling élite had a romance to it. And it was the kids' family holiday. It wasn't fair to cancel it. But for all her independence, she knew that she couldn't manage the children on her own. The long flight, the travelling they had planned, and the roughing it rather than hotels.

But then who could she ask? Her friends all had kids; all had husbands and family holidays planned. She could grovel to Andrew. Make it up.

But not this time. She knew he was right and it wasn't good for anyone to pretend anymore.

'Carl,' she said over breakfast. 'Carl. I've got a proposition for you.'

'Go on.'

'How do you fancy coming to Cuba with me and the kids?'

Carl was lounging at the table finishing off his fourth bowl of the kids' cereal. He was the lanky 25 year old son of a friend-of-a-friend who had yet to discover what he wanted to do with his life, and as he had teetered on the verge of fulfilling the stereotype of a South London young Black man, his mum had asked if he could have a term in the leafy suburbs away from temptation. But Jackie liked him. He was great with the children and quite tidy in a slightly obsessive but useful way.

'Great,' he said. 'Cool!'

And so that was that. She hadn't grovelled to Andrew. Hadn't made promises she couldn't keep. But she would still get her holiday, and three days later they all got up early for their trip.

'Vicky, stop brushing your hair and just get dressed!'

Toby came downstairs. Hat on and rucksack on his back, looking like a seasoned traveller.

'Can I just pop round to say good bye to Tom?' he said.

'You know you can't. Not yet. You're still only nine.'

'And I don't want to wear my trainers,' Vicky said, looking like she might throw herself prostrate on the floor at any moment.

Thankfully, Carl appeared, wearing his woolly hat as ever, and offered to take Toby and be back in five minutes. Jackie then managed to get Vicky dressed, checked for the second time that she had passports and tickets, then checked again that she had put them back after checking them, and zipped up the bags. As the taxi arrived, Carl and Toby came back and Andrew came out of the study to say good bye.

'He could have helped us get ready,' she thought, but realised that this was probably just a bit too unreasonable a thought to have, given the circumstances.

Two

'Wow! I'm in Cuba,' Jackie said as they got into a taxi. The guide book had said only get into licensed cabs, and don't be talked into getting into any old one, and here they were getting into any old one, but with a very nice looking man who had helped them with their bags. 'Whatever!' she thought.

The wall of heat had hit them at the airport and clothes had been peeled off and trainers exchanged for flip flops, whilst Jackie had got the special currency only available for tourists. And now in the taxi they all stared out of the windows.

'Look at those cars, darlings. They're old American cars from the 1950's. Still running. That's impressive!'

'They are all painted, mummy. Not shiny like ours. And look at that bird,' said Toby. 'It's enormous; must be a hawk or something.'

'Look there's another,' Jackie said. 'In fact, there's loads of them. Look at that tower. Hundreds of them circling around.'

'Mummy, look at that bus. Look how many people are in it,' said Vicky.

The taxi suddenly swerved to the left and the driver swore in Spanish.

'Blimey! That was a pot hole in the road. A massive one,' said Carl.

Soon they arrived in the old part of Havana, and after paying the driver, who seemed very happy with his money, they headed up to the large iron gate of where they were staying. The street was long and narrow on a steep hill that led up to a small stone church at the top, where two old blue Buicks were parked. They were going to travel around the island staying with families in rooms called 'Casa Particulars' where you could eat home cooked food, see how the locals lived and get a better insight into the real Cuba.

Their Casa turned out to be the top floor of a grand Spanish Colonial House. It had incredibly high ceilings, a winding marble staircase and an iron balcony around a central courtyard, which overlooked a combination of tropical plants, washing and plastic lobsters stuck onto the walls belonging to the family below. They were welcomed by a smiling man in shorts with a big pot belly, who showed them where they were to stay. There were two large rooms connected by a tall dark oak door, with wood panelled walls and marble floors and four beds covered in fine tapestries with tassels around the edges. A large wood and copper fan, which could have come from the Titanic, hung from the centre of the high ornate ceiling, and the furniture was made of delicately carved wood that was far too grand for the condition of the rest of the house. The whole place looked as if it had remained the same since the 1950s, except for the fridge and a metal air conditioning box which poked through a roughly cut hole in the wall. Ernesto, the owner, knocked on their huge wooden door and brought them four glasses of fruit juice.

'Mango,' he said, smiling. 'Cold. Welcome.' And they all sat down in the living room to chat in the universal language of hand waving, whilst they recovered from their journey.

'Mummy! It's got bits in it,' said Vicky.

'I don't like it,' said Toby. 'Can I have lemonade?'

'Mmm. I think it's lovely,' said Jackie making a point of drinking all three glasses.

She then smothered the children in sun cream, organised sun hats and water for their rucksacks and off they went into the hot and dusty street.

The buildings were all tall, old, grand and Spanish with pillars and plasterwork that had crumbled and would crumble more if you touched them. The streets were narrow and people everywhere were sitting in doorways or at glassless barred windows looking at the white people venturing into the heat. They could see marble, carvings and balconies as reminders of better days, but now washing filled the balconies and scrawny dogs sunned themselves on what was left of the doorsteps.

'Mummy, that dog's only got three legs,' said Vicky. 'Can we feed it?'

'Why are the dogs pink, mummy?' asked Toby. 'They've got no hair.'

They passed an old black man lying in a doorway with no shoes, either sleeping off the night before or just with nowhere better to go; a barber cutting a man's hair by the light from two fluorescent tubes that didn't seem to want to stay on, hanging from a wooden frame; and a pharmacist with empty shelves labelled 'medicines' and full shelves labelled 'vitamins'. And as they walked along, people quietly sidled up to them asking for money for their 'bambinos' or money just for themselves; and there were children everywhere in clothes that had been handed down once too often, holding their hands out for whatever might be on offer, all glancing around warily as they did so.

'Can we give them money, mummy? asked Toby.

'They are all black,' said Carl. 'I didn't realise they were all black. It's great. You stand out and I don't for once!'

They wended their way through the criss-cross of cobbled streets and turned to find the Cathedral with its huge entrance, towers and stone pillars - even more amazing than it looked in the guide books - and a square full of life, buzzing with music and talk.

'Ah!' said Jackie. 'Now, this is Cuba.'

Before Castro, Cuba had been governed by Batista and had become a two tier island for rich Americans and poor Cubans. Havana had been a hot bed of gambling, night clubs, fancy hotels and prostitution whilst the country side was full of Cubans working the fields with cattle-pulled machinery, bare feet and high levels of illiteracy. Castro had liberated Cuba in 1959 and his victory march into Havana had marked a time of hope for so many, with his promises of health care, education and the redistribution of wealth. Many of the rich investors had left for the US and Castro had quickly nationalised the banks, the land and the businesses. At a time when the US had been unashamedly toppling potentially communist governments across Latin America, the story of Castro, the charismatic Che Guevara and their band of rebels had the iconic qualities of good over evil and the survival and triumph of the underdog. And now, when all other leaders on a par with Castro had turned out to be corrupt, with their Swiss bank accounts revealed as they either fled, died or had been executed, Castro still seemed to be a decent man, who held on to his ideals and tried to live as he wanted others to. And Cuba was renowned for having an impressive number of doctors, and an extremely good, fully state-funded education system with very high levels of literacy. And for Jackie, embedded in her socialist consciousness, Cuba had always represented some sort of idealism and a possibility that people could live in a collective and caring way.

'You know, Toby,' she said 'When Castro was fighting Batista, at one point he only had two units left but rather than calling them Unit One and Unit Two he called them Two and Eight to convince Batista he had more. Isn't that clever? And when the US asked for them to open their borders,

Castro opened them for a week and sent all the criminals from his prisons to the United States. He's quite funny really'.

'What do you mean open their borders, mummy?' asked Vicky.

'Well, people in Cuba aren't allowed to leave Cuba. You know, like we go on holiday to France, Italy or even here. They have to stay in Cuba.'

'That's mean,' said Toby. 'He's mad.'

'It's because they have always been threatened by the US. Castro says they are under siege and that they all have to stick together. He says "you're either with us or against us".'

'You've got to admit,' said Carl 'That's a bit loopy. I bet Castro travels around when he wants to.'

'Not everyone wants to travel, you know. My Gran never left England'.

'But she could have,' said Carl under his breath.

'Right. Drink anyone?' and Jackie headed them off over to the beautiful restaurant in an old colonial mansion with its chairs and tables spilling out into the cobbled square.

They sat under their umbrella surrounded by cascading greenery which poured off the roof, drinking their icy drinks and listening to a band playing Cuban music. The musicians were all dressed in crisp white shirts and sheltered under the overhanging plants from the balcony of the restaurant. They played guitars, maracas and small drums and one scratched a stick across a hollow looking wooden tube whilst the singer sang 'Guantanamara' to them all. They were beautifully well rehearsed and their songs were flawless and Jackie gave them a large tip when they came round for their money.

'This is what I think of Cuba,' she said 'music and heat. Now all we need is rum.'

'Mummy,' said Toby 'can I go over there and see those painters?'

'Yes, darling, but don't go out of my sight. And take your sister,' she called after him as he set off.

Sitting in the shade along one side of the square was a line of men, all painting pictures of the Cathedral. They had small stools made of wood and were displaying their art on boards with clips. She watched her children wander off and chat to each of them looking at the pictures. Next time she looked, Toby and Vicky were sitting down alongside the others, drawing their own versions of the square.

'Hey look at that! I've got a couple of artists for children'.

'Mummy. This is Ralpho. He's using ink,' said Toby as Jackie wandered over. 'Can we buy them? Please.' Ralpho was only thirteen and spoke just a few words of English, but was very friendly with her and the children and quite a good draughtsman, having produced a series of very detailed drawings of the Cathedral.

'This is Oscar,' said Vicky 'He's helping me paint the Cathedral. Look. Watercolours'.

Oscar spoke excellent English and had a portfolio of water colours ranging from tourist friendly pictures of the square to abstract landscapes and seascapes. And of course he had a number of the standard paintings of Che Guevara which by now Jackie had realised were everywhere. He described how he had been a Salsa teacher, which was why he spoke such good English, and how he had heard that England was beautiful, but very cold, and how he didn't like the idea of being cold.

Jackie and Carl sat on the kerb with the artists and watched the square whilst the kids painted. The Cathedral stood impressively at one end with its pale stone façade, huge windows reflecting the light with their many colours, and doors open to the masses of tourists going in and out. Down one side was a building fronted with an arched walkway providing shade for the locals, and opposite was the restaurant with its tables and umbrellas for the tourists. And in the middle was the very life of the square. There were women wearing brightly coloured dresses with their hair held up high in coloured turbans, and a man wearing a Che Guevara T shirt with a huge grey beard, all smoking enormous Cuban cigars waiting to charge people for a photo opportunity. In the corner was a very large black woman, wearing a Miss Havisham-like white dress, laying out her cards to tell people their fortune. There was an ice cream seller pedalling his cart up and down in front of the Cathedral, and a wizened man sitting on the steps in the shade smoking a cigar, next to an international guide book showing him sitting on the steps, smoking a cigar, on its cover. And in the corner was a man with two woolly-hatted dogs in a pram that seemed to be able to understand his instructions. Then out of nowhere came the noise of a circus with drums and trumpets as a troop of performers on stilts marched into the square. They were all in silky shiny blue and red outfits and as they waded their way through the tourists they held out their buckets to collect money.

'They are amazing,' said Jackie. 'This country is amazing.'

And then, as the performers left the square, another band started to play; not the one with the crisp white shirts, but a small group of weather beaten wrinkled old men also sitting along the wall. They had maracas, a guitar and some drums like the others but they sat on small wooden boxes and one just brushed a tin lid along the pavement to keep time. And they sang like they had been singing all their lives. They sang heartfelt songs, romantic songs and songs that were for the soul not just for the tourists.

'Let's go out for dinner somewhere tonight, with music,' said Jackie. 'Oscar, how about you join us? Show us where to go?'

'That'd be great,' he said. And she noticed that not only was he completely beautiful, but that he looked at her for just a bit too long.

Three

'Vicky, your hair is lovely darling. Can you stop brushing it now and get dressed pleased?' Jackie said as they got ready for their first night out in Havana.

'Toby, have you cleaned your teeth?'

'Mummy,' said Toby 'Can I go and meet you there? I know where the square is'.

'No, darling. We're ready now. Let's all go together.'

She had put on her red dress and was wearing makeup, which she didn't usually bother with on holiday, and told herself that she was looking pretty good for 40. Carl had put his woolly hat back on, which seemed a bit unnecessary given that it was still about 30 degrees, but she kept quiet and decided that she didn't need to mother anyone else in her life. They said goodbye to Ernesto, who was sitting by the window at his black and gold sewing machine making crisp white shirts in the traditional style, and they headed off into the evening.

In Cuba there is very little dusk and the evening approaches in the style of 'daytime, bright orange sunset, pitch black', which can be shocking at first until you get used to the sun's sudden disappearance leaving nothing behind it. By the time they had reached the square, it was dark and the streets had all started to look the same.

They found Oscar sitting on the pavement as usual, with Ralpho who had nowhere else to go, and they were led off to a restaurant with tables outside. This was still in Old Havana but the buildings were less crumbled and looked as if they had been recently renovated. There was even a working fountain in the middle of the cobbled street with running water, and the streets were kept car free by three black cannons placed nose down into the concrete across the road. They sat down and looked at the menu, and the band who had been sitting at the next table got up to play their next set. The lead singer was blind and sang in the most wonderfully gentle voice whilst the other members moved effortlessly in their white shirts - possibly made by Ernesto.

'We can eat here and then go to a bar around the corner for dancing' said Oscar. 'It will start at about ten.'

'Can we stay up, mummy?' said the children together.

'I hope so,' said Jackie 'I feel like a late night.'

'Cool!'

Behind them was an elegantly tall building made of smooth sandstone with large wooden doors and clear glass windows showing the black of the night. A thin wrinkled man was sitting at the foot of the door wearing a white shirt, like the band, and jeans that were over-gathered at the waist to keep them up. He gently moved to the music.

'I want to paint him,' said Oscar. 'He's always here.'

And as the band changed to a new tune, the man stood up and started dancing on his own. His eyes were closed and his right arm clutched across his body to hold an absent lover and they swayed and swayed in perfect time with the music.

'He lives in a dream,' said Oscar.

'He looks stuck in the past,' said Jackie.

'But in a nice way,' said Oscar. 'I always think he is happy, not sad. Not a bad way to be; stuck in a happy past rather than in the present.'

They had their dinner whilst listening to the music, which ranged from classic Cuban salsa played rhythmically and passionately, to Cubanised versions of familiar songs, as tunes by the Beatles and Rolling Stones kept brushing through the beat. And they watched the old dancer in the corner dancing in a world that was no longer there.

Then it was time for salsa.

Oscar led the way to a bar with huge fans hanging from the ceiling, which did little to disperse the heat from the bodies that were starting to move to the music. A seven-piece band, wearing tight trousers and the ever present crisp shirts, occupied the middle of the room and energetically played, while the two lead men displayed fancy footwork in their white pointed shoes. The music was beginning to become familiar and Jackie could feel it starting to compete with the beat of her heart. Toby, Vicky and Carl sat eating their huge ice cream tubs whilst Ralpho drew sketches to colour in and Jackie and Oscar drank their Mojitos and watched as couples got up to dance.

'I can't salsa you know,' she said. 'I had lessons once with some friends but it was so hard. I could manage it without the music but sometimes the music is so fast.'

'I'll teach you,' said Oscar 'It's all about moving the body in the right way.'

But after many failed attempts at persuasion, Oscar took to the floor with a woman in a tight black dress and high heels, who understood what he meant about moving the body. And Jackie watched.

Salsa is a dance designed for confident men who know how to lead and women who are prepared to be led. But during her lessons in

England, Jackie and her friends had been reluctant to give up control, particularly to the English men in her class, who had been even more reluctant to take it. They had been taught how to count the salsa beat and how to carry out a basic number of moves that had started to look quite good. But when the music went on, the counting got confused and no one could decide which moves to do next. 'It's all in the hands,' the teacher had told them. 'The man leads by changing his hold on you, which signals what move he wants you to do.' But the men couldn't decide what move to do next and even when they managed to select whatever move came to mind, apart from muttering the words 'rumba', 'basic salsa' or 'spin' the hands-approach never seemed to work. And then the numbers of men started to dwindle, and standing out as an unaccompanied woman, as the remaining men worked their way around the circle, was just too reminiscent of school discos, so they had stopped going. But now Jackie wished she had persevered.

And she watched as Oscar took charge. He didn't count the beat, he felt it and he didn't seem to plan or decide or select what moves to do next, he just moved. And his bare black arms shone in the light with the heat, his hips moved and his body glimpsed through his damp shirt as he became one with the music. It was very sexy and

Jackie found herself taken off into a place of ceiling fans, thighs, sweat and muscles.

'Mummy, I'm tired,' said Toby out of nowhere.

'Oh! Yes you must be. I'd better get you home. You've been ever so good.'

'I'll take them if you like,' said Carl smiling at her. 'You can stay and enjoy the view for a bit longer.'

But Jackie gathered up the kids, said goodbye to Oscar and Ralpho, agreeing to take them to the beach the next day, and headed back to the Casa. And as they walked their way back up the hill, music could be heard coming from bars and restaurants and the open windows of apartments.

'It gets into your soul, this music,' Jackie said as she put the kids to bed. 'I'm so glad we came to Cuba.'

In the morning, they collected their modern hire car which had the luxury of air conditioning and seat belts, met up with Oscar and Ralpho and headed off to the beach. They had been told that Havana had three main beaches, two for Cubans and one for tourists and had decided to go native. As they turned out of the city on the beach road it seemed as if everyone else was heading for the beaches as well. The old American cars were crammed full of people with their feet and arms spilling out of the windows. They saw horse-pulled carts stacked with people wearing swimming costumes and carrying towels and the road side was packed with people waiting to hitch a lift. Even cattle trucks went past carrying people standing squashed all the way to the beach.

'Don't people have cars in Cuba?' asked Jackie.

'Not many. They used to before the revolution but now you only get a car if there is one passed down in your family. So we sort of share everyone else's cars.'

'And what about buses and trains?'

'We have them, but there aren't very many of them. Like two trains a week out of Havana. One bus each morning. Everyone just hitches.'

'A collective responsibility...?' said Jackie.

'Sort of,' said Oscar.

They arrived at the beach and parked the car alongside four old bangers and paid the attendant to keep an eye on it, as Oscar explained that the wheels might be gone if they didn't. Then they set off down to the sea. Jackie covered the kids in sun block, which felt even more necessary as they were obviously the only white children on the beach, and they headed down to jump in the sea which was like a large warm brown bath with gentle waves. Carl and Ralpho soon joined the children in the water and Jackie and Oscar settled themselves onto sun loungers in the shade. The beach was long and narrow with white pebbly sand and rocks and there was one café with a few straw umbrellas outside. No one looked like tourists and the Cubans sat around in large groups as their children played in the water. Along the edge of the sea was a line of men in green uniforms watching the swimmers. Oscar saw her looking.

'They are police. Checking no one escapes,' he said.

'No. Really?' said Jackie. 'What, swim off?'

'Yes. Every day people go to the US.'

'What, swimming? What about the sharks? Anyway, it's miles.'

'They try. They make boats, rafts, whatever they can to get away. So the police stand and watch.'

'What happens to the fishermen? Do they get watched?' asked Jackie.

'We have no fishermen. Not in boats anyway. The boats were banned. Now we have to fish from the beach.'

'But that's mad. This is an island. Fish must be your main source of food.'

'You'd have thought so, but Castro banned boats. After the 1990's when people escaped to Miami.'

'But I've eaten fish,' said Jackie 'We had fish last night.'

'You get it in state restaurants. The Casas can't give it to you - only chicken and pork.'

Jackie looked at him and then looked at the police and was quiet for a while.

'Oscar,' she said 'what's it like living here?'

He looked around him, nodded to the police and then looked straight back into her eyes. 'I'll tell you when you get back from your trip. When you let me teach you how to salsa,' he said. 'When we are alone and the music can drown it all out.'

Four

Getting out of Havana was a complicated process. There were no road signs showing either where the roads were going to, or which way the roads went, and it seemed incredibly dangerous to set off down a turning which could either join or leave the road you were on. This was exacerbated by the absence of any maps with any detail and the fact that anyone you asked for the 'auto pista' either answered in very fast Spanish or didn't drive, so had no idea where it was or how you might get there. Eventually, on their fourth time past the same junction, they stopped to ask a man by the side of the road, who spoke good English and pretty much begged for a lift as he was also going to Vinales, a small town in the mountains that was to be their next stop.

'It can take me three days this journey, you know. Sometimes I sit by the road for a whole day and no one stops. I tell my wife I'm on my way home but she never knows when I'm going to arrive'.

He was a tourist guide called Ricardo, although having just had an accident he was out of work at the moment. He sat in the front next to Jackie, with a huge rucksack on his knee, whilst Carl sat between the kids and played cards. Ricardo fortunately knew his way around the complex network of Havanan roads and with several turns in and out of junctions that no tourist would ever dare take, they were on the motorway heading west. The road was wide and smooth but it wasn't like any motorway that Jackie had ever seen. The road markings were so faded that the choice of lane was a random process, which was fine given that they seemed to be the only car in sight. And alongside what once had been the hard shoulder were cows tethered to stakes, people selling strings of onions with their vegetables laid out in piles on the floor and under every bridge were hordes of people sheltering from the sun whilst waiting to hitch a lift, hopefully to somewhere near their destination. And every now and again someone would cross the motorway to the other side, which filled Jackie with a surge of anxiety, even though the road was empty.

Ricardo found the new CD that Jackie had bought from the musicians in the Cathedral Square and put it on. Soon he was singing along passionately to every song and his eyes became moist as he waved his hands in time with the music.

'So wonderful!' he said. 'These are the songs of my childhood. So beautiful. My mother used to sing these to me.'

'Tell me about Cuba, Ricardo. Do you like living here?' Jackie asked after a while.

He started tentatively but within minutes was in a full scale rant. The privacy of the car and the passion of the music liberated him and he let it all out. He described how Cuba had been poor before the revolution and how Castro had redistributed the wealth but that was where the revolution should have ended. He said how they couldn't farm the land because all they had was a hoe and some cattle and how Castro wouldn't allow investment. He said the Communist party was corrupt and the high up members were the only rich people in Cuba and even the military were against Castro, so most of them were not allowed to carry guns to avoid a coup. He described how people were paid such low salaries and could never get a pay rise regardless of how hard they worked, and how the only money they could make was on the black market. And mostly he described his dream of being able to leave the island. 'It's like that film, 'Prisoner of Alcatraz.''

Jackie listened and interjected every now and again to try to get him back onto a more even keel.

'But you've all got jobs,' she said.

'Yes, but none of us is working. That's how we protest. You've seen them all standing around in bars. Doing nothing.'

'But you have so many doctors,' she said.

'But when we get to hospital there are no medicines.'

'And you are all so well educated,' she said.

'Educated and then we do nothing.'

'But before you were so poor.' she said.

'It's green,' he said, pointing out of the windows. 'Everywhere is green. We were never that poor.' Ricardo paused and looked at her. 'We just want what you have. That's all.'

After a while they put the music back on and Ricardo became calm whilst Jackie watched for potholes, and soon they arrived at the outskirts of Vinales. By now the landscape had completely transformed from low lying fields and rolling hills, to a wild and random assortment of mountains which looked like enormous boulders that had been dropped out of the sky. Jackie had told the children that they were going to the rainforest but it felt more like a very green and bumpy moonscape. The ever-present huge black birds were circling around, but now and then they saw enormous vultures with red heads eating the cadavers by the side of the road. And then suddenly it was raining. It was the first rain they had seen in Cuba and it was dramatic. The sky went black and the rain came down in a torrent bouncing off the road, turning the pavement into an instant river. People in the streets were ankle- then knee-deep in water and the car created waves that flooded the kerb. Then the lightning started and the kids squealed as forks of bright light shunted down into the ground in the mountains around them. They drove slowly into the centre of the town where the locals were sitting in their rocking chairs on their verandas watching the weather.

Unlike Havana, with its tall Spanish colonial mansions, the people of Vinales lived in single storey, box like houses, each in the middle of its own small plot of land and each with two windows at the front and a door in the middle. The houses were all different colours and the streets reminded Jackie of the rows of beach huts found in traditional English seaside resorts. Ricardo had told them that he had a friend with a room to rent and soon they found the house on a hill with its veranda at the top of concrete steps having a spectacular view across the mountains. The house turned out to have three rooms and an open-plan living area and kitchen. The family all lived in the front room and the back two rooms were for guests. Jackie and the kids settled into one room, which was just big enough for two double beds with a small table sandwiched between them, and they piled their bags up against the wall as there was nowhere to unpack their clothes. The room had one glassless window which was covered by wooden shutters and a brightly patterned curtain which also hung around the other walls, giving the room the feel of a den made by children who had just gained access to a sewing machine. There was also an air conditioning box posted through a hole in the wall and a tiny bathroom, with just enough room to turn around between the sink, toilet and shower and the increasingly familiar bin to put used toilet paper in which Jackie felt was the one part of Cuba she could never get used to. They then went out onto the veranda to watch the lightning where the air was much cooler and more manageable since the storm. The rain was still pouring out of the sky, bouncing off the steps up to their house and hitting the large shiny leaves of the plants in the garden. The hammering noise was strangely peaceful and it was like sitting in a children's drawing with artificial unnatural lines of light hitting the world around them and enormous mountain-like clouds.

Then suddenly it all stopped. The silence returned and the heat set in, causing the ground to steam around them.

'Let's go for a walk,' said Jackie 'and check out the town.'

Toby needed persuading, as he had settled into yet another game of cards, and Vicky complained that it was muddy and wet and there would be nothing new to see. But eventually they were convinced and wandered up a narrow track away from the main road.

The house they were staying in was made of brick, rendered in white plaster and looked solidly built, suggesting money of some sort. But as soon as they got two houses up the path, things changed. The houses were still of the same double fronted design, but some were made of wood, many had gaping cracks in the walls and one was just a few rows of rubble. There were pigs tethered to trees, pigs just wandering around, chickens plucking themselves and each other and the occasional small horse tethered to a stake in the ground. In front of one wooden house, stood a smooth brown horse eating the grass and an even smoother browner man brushing him down. He had his shirt off and was wearing army green trousers, and his black moustache and smooth black hair gave him the air of a young and wilder Clark Gable. He waved and smiled and walked the horse down to meet them. After a short exchange of bad Spanish from Jackie, which sounded more like basic French with a's on the end, they found out that his name was Danielle, and the children took turns to ride the horse as he walked them up and down the path. They said 'thank you' but as they were walking off he came out with a couple of large cages.

'Wow!' said Vicky 'What are those?'

Inside the cages were two large brown animals which looked either like hairy beavers without the flattened tail, or giant rats. The creatures were both eating bits of sweet corn and oblivious to the excitement they had just created in the two strange, pale children.

'Tree rats,' said the man. 'Boy, girl.'

He then took them up to his house and through to the back yard. As they walked down the side alleyway they could see rooms full of beds, glassless windows with broken shutters and a number of people of all different ages, who by the time they had got to the yard had made their way outside to meet them. There seemed to be about eight people living in the house of four rooms, who must have been several generations of an extended family. There were two other men, older than Danielle, who looked like friendly Mexican bandits smoking cigarettes, and two little girls about the same age as Vicky, who stood coyly at the doorway in their flip flops. In the garden, there was a large shed on stilts and Toby and Vicky climbed up the ladder of branches to find pigeons with extra large heads in cages. The children squealed as they were allowed to hold them, and one by one Danielle threw them up into the air. The pigeons flew up onto the nearest roof then after a couple of whistles, made their way obediently back into their cages. They seemed quite content to do this over and over to please the children and showed no desire to fly off and escape. The air in the shed was feathery and thick and the heat was trapped but the children took the pigeons in and out of their cages, launching them into the air and practised capturing them over again.

Next, Danielle showed them the rest of his animal collection. He had two more tree rats in cages by the back door step, a goat tied up in a small stick-made cage and two piglets and their mother on long leashes under the tree. He also had a small plastic tank with fishes in and a scrawny dog that followed them around. The two young girls giggled as they watched the foreign children get so much excitement from their world, and a woman, about Jackie's age, sat on the step being as welcoming as is possible without having to say anything.

'You eat?' said Jackie pointing to the pig and signing the universal language.

'Yes,' nodded one the of Mexican men rubbing his stomach

'Mmm!'

'You eat?' said Jackie and she pointed to the tree rats.

'Yes,' he said again laughing.

'Eat?' pointing at the fish.

'Yes.'

'Eat?' pointing at the goats.

'Yes.'

'Eat?' said Toby pointing at the scrawny dog.

'No,' laughed the man pulling a face 'errr'.

'Well, why not?' said Toby. 'I would'.

They all laughed as Toby continued to explain that it was mad to eat everything else and not dogs, whilst Vicky stroked the dog in a protective way. After more time to check the pigeons and feed grass to the pigs, Jackie and the children wandered back to find Carl asleep on the veranda and their hostess cooking dinner in the kitchen. Jackie sat down on the other rocking chair and within seconds the kids had disappeared to explore. The house overlooked the road into the town, and she could see a row of verandas with people rocking and watching the world go by. She could hear some pigs snuffling and distant giggling of children and wondered for a moment if she should check on the kids, but decided instead to get her book and curl up for a read.

Five

The following morning they woke to several cockerels going off at once, to find that the rest of the family were up and about and had all slept in. Toby rushed into his clothes and disappeared off, whilst Jackie and Vicky tidied up the room which seemed to have suffered bomb damage even though they had only been there a day. By the time they emerged, the table was set for four with an elaborately embroidered table cloth and napkins and they settled down to what was becoming a familiar routine of a fresh egg omelette with or without sausage, a jug of fresh fruit juice made from the mango or pineapple tree in the garden, white bread which was like very large French baguettes and then a plate of sliced fruit including very small bananas. Jackie, who had eaten a slice of toast and marmite every morning for her breakfast ever since she could remember, found it all a bit overwhelming but ate as much as she could to avoid any waste, whereas Toby and Carl finished their lot within minutes. Vicky sat on her chair chatting away eating the middle out of the white bread drizzled with honey, leaving the rest of her portion to Carl to shovel down.

As their hostess was tidying away, Jackie tried to ask her where the food came from, as so far they hadn't seen any food shops, but her Spanish wasn't up to it and even with the phrase book the woman became confused and looked like she might think Jackie was complaining. So she gave up, smiling and trying to look very pleased with everything. Then she went off to find the kids so they could start their day. She found Vicky feeding grass to the pigs at the front of the house in her bare feet, and after much calling Toby appeared on the roof of the house looking over the edge grinning happily.

'They've got pigeons as well mummy,' he said 'Up here. The boy has let me hold them.'

'How did you get up there darling? Is it safe?' asked Jackie.

'Yeah, yeah, yeah. Stop worrying. There's a ladder at the back. Come up.'

A tall teenage boy appeared over the side of the roof, holding a pigeon which he promptly threw into the air and Vicky squealed as it flew over her head and landed on a post nearby.

'Mummy. Can we have pigeons? Please. I could build a shed in the garden. Or even on our roof,' said Toby.

'And can we have pigs or chickens?' said Vicky.

'Your great granddad used to have pigeons, you know. He loved it' said Jackie.

Jackie gave up on her plans to spend the morning in town, after failing to persuade the children to leave the house, and sat back in a rocking chair to read her book. The children were now nine and seven, and Jackie had spent most of those years trying to be a good mother, which had involved playing, reading and talking with her children all the time when she wasn't at work. As a result they still expected her to be involved in whatever they were doing and she sometimes wondered if her enthusiasm had created two very high-maintenance children. And sitting on the veranda, in the sun, on her own, holding her own book, she realised that she hadn't done this for a long time. She was reading Fidel Castro's autobiography which was a big thick tome and involved the transcription of several long interviews with him by a South American journalist. The book had a large photo of Castro on its cover, in his familiar army combats, and inside were several pictures of him with famous authors such as Ernest Hemmingway, and world leaders including, Nelson Mandela and Gorbechev. There were also numerous photos of Che Guevara who seemed such a clever and honest man and reminded her of her student days when so many of her friends had had the iconic image of him on their walls. All those demonstrations she had been on: the marches, the sit-ins, the trips to London to protest outside the Houses of Parliament. All trying to preserve the nationalised industries and to create a better world of free education and health care and one where the poor were looked after. Perhaps occupying the arts building on campus wasn't really going to stop the closure of the coal mines but at least she had felt that they were doing their bit.

'Mummy. Look what I've got,' said Toby excitedly.

He was standing in front of her holding a long piece of grass and with its head through a loop at the end hung a large green and blue lizard.

'It's a chameleon,' he said 'I caught it. The boy showed me how to catch it. I made this knot in the end and I waited around the corner of the wall and then just got it.'

He carefully put it down on the table with its head in the noose and as it breathed, a bright red bubble of skin inflated on its neck.

'There're loads of them everywhere you look. On the walls. In the bushes. Some are tiny. This was the biggest.'

Vicky then came over with the two girls from Danielle's house and they all stood looking at the lizard, although the girls were more interested in Toby and Vicky.

'We've been feeding the pigs and the goats, mummy,' said Vicky. 'And I held a pigeon.'

'And, mummy, Danielle wants to know if we want to go up into the mountains with him?'

They wandered over to find Danielle on his front step smoking a cigarette, and after even more grass was fed to the pigs and more pigeons were thrown into the air it was agreed that they would head off into the mountains as soon as possible to avoid the heat and the afternoon's rain. They rushed back to their house and Jackie watched as Vicky put on her new long trousers which she had said she hated, her new long sleeved T-shirt which she'd said had itched, and trainers and socks which had been the source of many sticker charts over the years, without a murmur. She even succumbed to her hat, which was also usually a major source of conflict, and they set off with Danielle in the car. Carl had decided to stay behind and have a sleep and Danielle sat in the front next to Jackie wearing his wide brimmed hat, with his elbow out of the open window enjoying the ride, and they didn't have the heart to tell him about the air conditioning or that he should put his seat belt on.

Soon they turned off the road to find two houses in a field and Danielle told them to stop the car. The first house was very similar to the one they were staying in with white render and two windows at the front on either side of the coloured door. The second was made of wood with wide gaps between the planks and a woman came out to greet them. She turned out to be Danielle's aunt and she kissed him, shook Jackie's hand warmly and ruffled the kids' hair. She had a huge water tank at the front of the house full of greenish water, while pigs and chickens wandered around. Her neighbour came out of her house and invited them to look inside where she proudly showed them the TV, the music centre and the cooker.

'What a lovely house' said Jackie.

'Yes' she said 'Cool. Nice and cool. Next door is hot,' she said, pointing.

Jackie wanted to ask why there was so much difference in the way people lived; how some people had so much more than others; how you bought a new house; how you got a job? But her lack of Spanish meant that she just smiled and admired what she was being shown. Danielle then led them through a field of sweet corn and suddenly they were in a wide green opening with a huge boulder-like mountain ahead of them fronted by a sheer rock face painted in bright blues and greens.

'Mummy. Look it's a dinosaur,' said Vicky. 'Did they have dinosaurs here?'

'I guess so darling,' said Jackie. 'That's really peculiar.'

The rock face was covered in a gaudy painting of massive Tyrannosaurus Rexes and plant eaters, which belonged on the front of a children's magazine rather than on a mountainside. Yet behind it was a green and beautiful landscape with soaring black birds that looked as if it had been untouched for thousands of years.

'Why would someone do that?' asked Jackie. 'It's really out of place.'

'Castro,' said Danielle. 'Big! After revolution.'

Apart from the shock of the mural, the rest of their trip turned out to be an adventure into nature. Danielle took them to the foot of the mountain, and as they looked up their view was blocked by thick green foliage, as vines, branches and leaves wound across a narrow overgrown path. And then they started to climb upwards, bit by bit, up to the top. They scrambled on hands and knees over broken trunks and through the rocks, finding tricky foot holes to haul themselves up. They climbed wooden rickety ladders held on by rope, to help when the path became vertical. And they held on to branches for leverage or were pulled up by the arm with legs dangling in mid-air by Danielle, who turned out to be extremely strong. Their clothes stuck to them in the heat and the knees on their trousers made it hard for their legs to bend, but they were all determined to look as much like natives as they could. Jackie's hair was matted to her head, and she could feel insects burrowing into the back of her neck, but she decided to picture herself more as the Amazonian woman than a sweaty tourist, which gave her that extra edge to carry on.

By the time they got to the top Toby and Vicky were wide-eyed and very hot but hadn't moaned once and they all slumped down onto a rock. The birds were now beneath them and seemed massive with their outspread wings and they could see down over the mural across to the distant houses they had been in earlier. They were high above a plain and around them were numerous similar separate mountains looking like they had been dropped out of the sky. Everywhere was green and alive and yet very little looked like it was being farmed in any way.

'Hey mummy, look,' said Toby.

Jackie turned round to find Danielle grinning with a lizard hanging off his ear clinging on by its teeth.

'Ow! Does that hurt?'

'Can I do that mummy?' asked Toby.

'I don't know darling,' she said.

But Danielle carefully prised the lizard off his ear and attached it to Toby's, who stood very still trying not to laugh too much. Then it was Vicky's turn and Danielle hunted around in the leaves so that she could have two.

The trip down the mountain was faster but harder as their knees jolted at every step and their toes banged the front of their shoes. Danielle lifted the children down the steeper drops and dangled them down the ladders feet first, and his strength made Jackie feel like the delicate soul she had never been, when he held onto one of her arms as she lowered herself down. Danielle showed them more lizards, which when they looked turned out to be everywhere, and pointed out brightly coloured birds in the trees and a frog that disappeared into its surroundings. Then at the bottom he took them off to see some caves.

By now they were in the flat plain at the foot of the mountains, which was partly farmed to grow sweet corn. He pulled off cobs for them to eat straight from the bush, pointed out plants that were good for tooth ache if you chewed them and those that were good for stomach ache if you ate them. They saw a revolting huge jelly animal which turned out to be a giant millipede about the length of an adult's hand and they saw trees growing bananas, mangoes, papayas and small green fruits which were full of seeds. At each new tree Danielle got out his knife from the sheath in his belt and cut down something new for them to try and Jackie watched as her children were keen to sample everything.

Then they were at the caves.

Anywhere else in the world, caves are entered via a ticket stand, a gift shop, a detailed health and safety warning, guide books and an audio tour. These were accessed by a rusty broken ladder propped up between the ground and a gap in the mountain side which took them into the entrance of an amazing series of openings with water and rock formations everywhere. The ceilings were littered with stalactites of all different sizes, and yellowed ribbons of rock covered the walls. There were huge cavernous holes in the floor that they had to avoid and passageways leading off, both up and down, into other even darker places. Jackie missed not having any information about how old the caves were, when they were found or how they were formed, but standing in the pitch black with the walls lit by Danielle's lighter and then having Danielle shockingly snap off some stalactites for the children to take home, gave the caves a meaning all of their own.

They set off back to the car more slowly than before as the sun was now directly above them. Everyone's hair stuck to their heads and they flapped their T-shirts to make the most of any coolness left in the air. Even Danielle was glowing as if he might wilt soon. .They walked past pigs, dogs and bony cows with big horns which kept the children amused, but by the time they got back to the car they were all ready to wind up the windows, put the air conditioning on full blast and get back for their lunch. Organising payment to Danielle was difficult as he wanted to give their hostess half of whatever they offered as she had introduced them to him. Yet Jackie wanted to give him enough to show what a fantastic time they had had and eventually she gave him a sum of money which made his grin even wider than usual.

The next two days were the closest to a relaxing holiday that Jackie had had since having children. She spent most of her time sitting on the veranda reading, whilst Carl either slept or wandered off on his own and the kids played with the locals or fed the animals. As a child, Jackie had lived in a small semi detached house backing onto an alley way and she and her sister had spent most of the time squeezing in and out of people's gardens, climbing onto garage roofs and making dens with whoever was around. Her mum had always said that she had been desperate for some space to herself but looking back, mothering in those days looked like a much more hands-off activity. The roads were quieter and the threat of the local weirdo had seemed much less of a possibility and most of Jackie's memories of her mum were of her standing in the back garden calling them in for tea. Jackie had a scar on her foot from falling off her bike and having the pedal knock a block off her skin. The woman from up the road had found her crying and brought her home. But the bike had been one of those tricycles with pedals fixed to the wheels that keep going round even when you stop pedalling and the woman had lived two roads away. She must have been about three years old; only three, and at the end of this woman's road on her own. She had told this to her sister recently, who had pointed to her own scar caused by putting her teeth through her bottom lip, also a result of riding the same bike and being brought home by a different friendly neighbour from the top of the main road into town. Jackie could also remember going to the lido with her friends by bus and jumping out at passersby in the local woods dressed as an old woman. She wasn't sure exactly how old she had been but she had been with friends she hadn't seen since she was ten. And this wasn't in some quiet village in the middle of nowhere. They had been brought up in a suburb of London. Yet Jackie's children were always close at hand. They played in the park, they rode their bikes and they went swimming, as Jackie was determined that they should have an outdoor life, but she was always either sitting on a bench nearby chatting with a friend drinking endless tea or on her own bike racing them to the next stopping place. It wasn't that she didn't want them to grow up. It wasn't even that she was particularly worried about cars or scared of weirdoes. It was more that she couldn't bring herself to be the first to let her children have the freedom they desperately wanted. No other mums let their children out and about and so she followed suit. All the other mums took their kids to school so she did as well. The fear of something dreadful happening was obviously scary. She felt that in reality the risks were small but the fear of being blamed, feeling guilty and being seen as a terrible mum made it just not worth taking even these small risks. But two days in the mountains in Cuba and she had read half a book and her children were nowhere to be seen.

That evening after trying to eat as much as possible of their enormous dinner, they were sitting around the table finishing off their drinks when Danielle appeared at the door to say that he had something new to show the children. He looked particularly cheeky and when they arrived at his house he got out a box and put it on the table. The children huddled around whilst his family watched, smiling. Suddenly an enormous spider emerged from the box, about the size of an adult hand with black hairy legs and a thick body, and ran off to the sound of shrieks and squeals from the kids and laughter from everyone else.

'You like?' said Danielle, grinning.

'What was that?' said Jackie. 'It looked like a tarantula'

'Not dangerous,' said Danielle and chased the spider off into the bushes.

The air was still thick with heat but the birds had now gone and as the last of the light disappeared one of the Mexican men pulled up a wooden chair for Jackie and came to sit next to her. Danielle then joined them and soon all the family were out on the veranda with Jackie, listening to music from a small cassette player. The children wandered off around the back of the house with the two girls to explore in the dark whilst the adults were left to sing, clap and stamp their feet in time to the Cuban music that Jackie was beginning to own.

'You dance?' asked one of the Mexicans.

He stood in front of her with his arm outstretched. His hair was thick and black and the contrast with his blue eyes was striking.

He had a moustache similar to Danielle's but his face was more lined and more weathered; more direct and more experienced.

'Oh No! No No!' said Jackie.

But her protests were ignored and he pulled her to her feet and firmly began to move her around. Two others then got up and danced and the woman sang whilst Danielle beat out the rhythm on a cow skin seat. At first Jackie was aware she was being watched and tried to keep the salsa beat as she had been taught in her classes, but the night was warm and the sky was black and the strong arms and determined movements enabled Jackie to slip into the role of a sensual woman dancing with her lover. She could feel his body through his shirt and his hard muscles moved under her hands. He smelled of nature, without the chemicals of English men, and his neck became damp as they moved. His knees pushed through hers and his palms pressed to the crook of her back pulling her hips into his. When she held his hands they slipped, when she touched his back he fitted into her and as his shirt rode up with the movements she placed her hand on his wet skin below and her fingers drifted into the belt of his trousers. They laughed when she got the steps wrong and he stared deep into her when it was right. And when he spun her round the air cooled on her face and her children and her life in England seeped away. She became herself again and it was like welcoming back a lost and wonderful friend. Transformed, she sat down to drink what tasted like a rum and coke.

'You like Cuba Libre?' asked Danielle pointing to her glass.

'It's wonderful,' she said. 'Perfect'.

Six

The next morning they said goodbye to their hosts and to Danielle and his family, dishing out Vicky's clothes and colouring pens to the girls and Carl's T-shirts to the men, then set off on their journey to their next planned destination, Trinidad. Trinidad is a city further East on the island and is a designated World Heritage centre known for its architecture, which has remained unchanged since the 18th century. They were also planning to stop off at a crocodile farm to keep the children amused before exposing them to more old buildings. They drove through the mountains and were quickly on the main road where the familiar hitch-hikers could be seen lining the sides.

By now Jackie felt it was unethical to have an empty seat in the car so they picked up a series of people wanting short lifts, including an elderly man who stared straight ahead clutching his bag and refusing to enter into any hand waving or signing attempts, and a young girl of about 14 who was fascinated by the phrase book and wanted to practise as much English as she could before she got out by a flyover. Toby and Vicky were shocked that such a young person could be out hitching on her own and they watched her walking up the sides of the steep motorway cutting onto another main road to catch a lift for the next part of her complicated journey. They then picked up a man in his forties called Enzo, who spoke excellent English and was overwhelmed with gratitude to find out that they were going all the way to Trinidad where his family were waiting for him.

'How do they know when to expect you?' asked Jackie, thinking how difficult it would be if Andrew didn't walk through the door at 6.10 every night to find his dinner on the table.

'They don't really,' he said 'they just wait.'

'Can you call them?' she asked.

'When I leave, but not after that.'

'But I've read you have mobile phones now,' she said.

'Ah! That would be nice,' said Enzo. 'How much do they cost in England?'

'About £50 - about 4 hours work.'

'In Cuba - about 4 months' work,' he said. 'They say we can have them but they are too expensive. Like the internet.'

'But I thought you had that now,' said Jackie.

'We do. But we can't afford to use it.'

'But you have international TV now?' she said 'I read that in the papers.'

'Not really. Only in the tourist hotels. Too expensive for Cubans.'

Enzo rummaged through his bag and pulled out a letter in a white envelope from an English couple who had been travelling in Cuba. He read the letter out, which said that they hoped the T-shirts fitted and that the phone worked.

'They sent me a phone from England,' he said. 'The T-shirts were fine but the phone never got here. Castro. He can talk, but he doesn't like us doing it.'

'What! They nicked it?' said Toby, who was becoming an expert at listening in on adult conversations.

'The box was sealed but they must have taken it.'

He paused, looked at the letter and then carefully put it back into its envelope.

'Castro is a thief. And he's a liar.'

Jackie looked across at him and could see the anger written in the lines on his face.

'I've been reading his autobiography,' she said. 'I always thought he was a decent man. That he wanted what was best for the Cubans and was incorruptible.'

'Ha!' sneered Enzo. 'He did in the beginning. He was a great man. Cuba needed the revolution.

We needed him otherwise we would have just stayed as a US puppet, but he changed. He aligned himself with Russia and then Che Guevara died. Once he had gone there was no one left to speak up to him. We were supposed to be independent but then we became a Russian pet. Their poor pet. How can you have self respect when you are just the pet of another country?'

'And Che Guevara?' Jackie asked. 'Was he a good man?'

'The best,' said Enzo 'A very clever man, a man of honour.'

'His picture is everywhere,' said Jackie 'He is like your God.'

'If he had lived we would have been a good country. He spoke up to Castro. He knew how the country should be managed.'

'So the Americans killed him?' said Jackie.

'Yes. They killed him. And Castro could do whatever he wanted.'

'They have a bad history, the Americans,' said Jackie.

'But how did they know where he was?' asked Enzo 'Why had he gone to Bolivia? There was no war there.'

'I thought he was spreading the word of the revolution,' said Jackie.

'Castro sent him,' said Enzo, spitting the words out. 'And told the CIA where he was.'

'He had him killed?' said Toby. 'But they were friends. All those pictures of them together.'

'And Cienfuegos? What happened to him? He was another powerful man. He went off in a plane and was never seen again,' said Enzo.

They all looked at him in silence.

'Castro had them both killed. Too many powerful men. Not enough room in Cuba for all of them.'

Jackie had come to Cuba prepared. She had watched films about Che Guevara's trips around South America and the Cuban missile crisis and she had read Ernesto Guevara's biography of his son's life. And now she had even managed to wade through half of Castro's autobiography. She felt she had an understanding of Cuban history, its politics and its place in the world as a small island fighting for independence so close to the biggest power in the world. And what Enzo was telling her didn't feel right. Maybe he knew something that had been kept from the rest of world or perhaps he was just an embittered man thriving off his own conspiracy theory. For the first time since she had left for Cuba, Jackie thought of Andrew. Andrew understood world affairs better than her. In fact he had a much broader grasp of most things than her and she needed him to be here now; to hear what Enzo was saying and to help her decide what to think. When they had first got together she loved his extensive knowledge of everything and it had been great to learn by talking over dinner rather than wading through dry books of fact. But over recent years his role as the family human encyclopaedia had began to annoy her. She no longer turned to him to explain the latest downturn in the market or the elections in other parts of the world but preferred either to remain ignorant or to glean what she could from her brief glances at the paper. Asking him only seemed to feed a dynamic in their marriage that no longer worked for her. She wanted to be an adult but his knowledge made her into the child; and she wanted her independence but his explanations made her feel controlled. But now, it would have been good to talk all this through.

They carried on their long journey making polite conversation and Jackie watched Cuban life pass her by at the side of the motorway. There were cows, people selling onions and fruit, the familiar hitchhiker everywhere, and every now and again they passed a cattle truck or an old American car crammed full of people. Then, there was an almighty bang, the car dipped and swerved and she struggled to regain control.

'What was that?' shouted Carl from the back seat. 'Did we hit a pot hole?'

It soon became obvious that they had lost a tyre as the wheels started to rattle and the car dragged, bumping them over to the side of the road. Jackie managed to take the car off the main road onto what must have once been the hard shoulder, and they all got out to assess the damage.

Jackie prided herself on being independent. She paid her way in the family, had decorated their houses over the years and could even turn her hand to rewiring. But she had never changed a wheel and felt both irritated and relieved when Enzo took charge, found the jack and spare wheel in the boot of the car and finished within minutes.

'Thanks Enzo,' she said as they got back into the car 'Don't know how I would have managed that without you.'

'I could have done it,' said Carl from the back seat.

'Oh yeah!' Toby and Vicky said together.

'You know, in our country,' said Enzo turning to Toby in the back 'your mother is the one who you love and who looks after you. But your father. Well, he's the one you turn to when things go wrong. If you have a problem or a question, then it's your father who will always know the answer. We all love our mothers but fathers are always the rock we can rely upon. You should always remember that.'

Jackie looked at Toby and realised that she now definitely needed Andrew to be there. Andrew might know more than her, but he had always treated her with respect and would certainly never have dared to be so patronising. She then looked at Enzo and decided he might well be helpful, and she was grateful that he had changed the wheel, but he was an old fashioned embittered bigot who was not only wrong about Castro but also wrong about everything else as well.

The drive was long, the children were bored and there was a tension from Jackie that filled the car. But after some complicated navigation by Enzo, due to the absence of road signs anywhere, they arrived at the crocodile farm which had been used as bait for several miles to keep the children going.

'Hurrah! We're here!' cheered Jackie as they turned into a modern looking car park containing more coaches and foreign cars than they had seen all holiday.

They piled out into the heat of the afternoon and headed off towards the entrance that was marked in English and Spanish.

'It feels odd to see English again,' said Jackie 'I've got used to not really understanding anything.'

Jackie paid an enormous amount for them all to go in, using her tourist money, and noticed that Enzo was on one side talking to a man in uniform. There were signs everywhere in English offering drinks, guide books, postcards and food and one advertised 'crocodile burgers' which seemed strange given that the farm had been set up as a conservation area to protect Cuban crocodiles from extinction. Enzo joined them and explained that he had had to say that he was their guide otherwise he wouldn't have been allowed in.

'This is a tourist attraction,' he said 'Cubans aren't good enough to come here.'

They set off to see the crocodiles. The guide books recommended the farm as a 'must see' event and the full car park suggested that it was a popular place to come, but Jackie felt increasingly despondent as they walked around a large lake looking at crocodiles through a high wire fence. There were plenty of crocodiles as expected and they were in a relatively natural environment as the book said, but whether it was knowing that it was just for tourists, or the possible prospect of eating one of them at the end of their day, the visit didn't have the impact on her that she had hoped. Toby and Vicky loved it and spotted pairs of eyes as they emerged out of the surface of the water. Carl was the most animated he had been all holiday and kept pretending to grab the kids from behind making roaring noises, even though Toby pointed out that it was lions that roared not crocodiles.

But very soon, and much sooner than was justified by the amount it had cost to get in, the visit was over and they were getting back in the car, as Jackie made a note to herself to avoid tourist attractions in future. Enzo then found their way back onto the main road and they arrived in Trinidad around dinner time with very tired and irritated children and Carl fast asleep as usual.

Seven

They spent their first night in Trinidad in a small Casa and then ventured out into the town after breakfast to explore their new base. The geometric grid of streets was narrow and densely packed with terraces of single storied houses painted in the remnants of blues, greens and pinks. Most doors were open with steps leading straight onto the pavements which quickly dropped down to the cobbles below and it looked as if the town had remained unchanged for centuries apart from the flaking paint and the odd fluorescent tube hanging above some of the windows. They saw people sitting on steps, people looking out of their windows and people passing by on bicycles: and everywhere, people were trying to sell them whatever they had to sell. Inside windows old clothes, toys and pots and pans were laid out for customers to see, and along the pavement men stood guarding their stocks of a few light bulbs, some matches and a coil of wire or string.

They walked up towards the main square, and as they did so the sun rose in the sky and it became hotter than it had ever been before. The roads were dusty, the air was thick and sticky and the buildings seemed to trap the heat just where they were walking. And nothing seemed to help. Wafting the fans they had bought from the side of the road, flapping their shirts and blowing on each others' necks failed to generate any relief as the air refused to be cooled and remained stuck and unmoved. Even the Cubans hovered in doorways and the tourists could be seen inside the cafés claiming the fans and the cold drinks. They walked down a market street with stalls on either side selling cloth dolls which were either white or black depending on which way up they were held, beautiful lace work fashioned into clothes or sold as table cloths, and wooden carvings of slaves and their shackles or musicians and their instruments. But they were too hot to look and the invitations to touch or try from the stall holders felt overwhelming and intrusive.

'Mummy I feel ill,' said Toby.

'I can't walk anymore, mummy. It's horrible here,' said Vicky.

'It's beautiful darlings but it is too hot,' said Jackie. 'I'm melting.'

So they staggered back to their car, closed the windows, turned on the air conditioning and sat back to cool down.

Carl listened to his music and the kids lolled about the back seat whilst Jackie read through the guide book trying to decide how they should spend their day. In her twenties Jackie had spent most of her holidays lounging by swimming pools reading books and chatting to French and Dutch men on various campsites across France. As a result, by the time she met Andrew she was extremely well read but hadn't seen much of the world. So their holidays before the children arrived had been driven by her desire to make up for lost time and they had seen as many cathedrals, temples and ruins as it was possible to see in a time-limited summer holiday. They had also agreed that it was important to visit places that were going to change and had managed to get to the Far East and parts of Africa. Since having children, however, they had returned to the campsite model of holidays, but paddling had replacing reading and a quick chat about the day after the kids had gone to sleep had taken the place of any chance of a flirtation with the locals. Now the kids were older and Cuba was to have been their attempt at merging family life with a desire to see cultures on the move. But it was hot and there was probably a limit to how many old buildings you could expect children to appreciate.

'Let's go to the seaside,' she announced.

'Yeah!' everyone else in the car said together. 'Brilliant idea!'

And two hours later they had found a new Casa in a small fishing village with a pebbly beach and palm trees moving in a way that promised relief from the heat. Their new hosts were a couple who spoke excellent English and owned a beautiful white house with a veranda all the way around and a garden full of trees laden with every kind of the tropical fruits they had tasted so far. It was separated from the beach only by a small road and they quickly unpacked their bags into their tiny rooms and headed off down to the sea.

In the guide books there were photos of expansive Cuban beaches with white sand, palm trees, blue seas and water sports with people sunning themselves or sheltering on recliners under parasols made of reeds. And the people were all white. Here, the sand was grey and stony, full of weed and littered with rubbish and the only shade was from a few trees or in the shadow of the wall that ran along the road. But the brown sea was alive with families standing around waist high, some holding umbrellas, some smoking and all chatting, laughing and playing with their kids. This was a Cuban holiday village and Jackie was pleased to be off the tourist track again. They laid their towels along the wall for Carl to lie down on and Jackie took the children to the sea.

Jackie had taken the kids swimming for years with the belief that one day they would be able to play safely on their own leaving her to read her book or just stare out over the water and ponder her life. But she had never liked it and had stood there week after week in cold thigh deep water with one or other of them clinging on to her thinking of the good mothering points she was collecting and wondering if she really was the only woman left in Surrey with pubic hair. And this wasn't helped by an irrational fear of sharks that seemed perfectly rational to her and had been caused by seeing the film 'Jaws' at a vulnerable age. As a child she had spent many a bath time watching the plug hole in a case a large rubber model squeezed its way through, and as an adult the desire to leave the water could be triggered by the random onset of the thumping music in her head. But now her children wanted to go in the sea so she felt duty-bound to take them and to make a show of enjoying it. But the water was warm, there was no shock to the system as it passed up her body, the sea bed was sandy and it only ever seemed to get waist deep. There were also so many other people much further out than her that she felt convinced that any shark would get them before her. The children wanted to swim out to a rock but she managed to keep them close and they played around in the water with Jackie trying to enjoy being splashed and climbed all over and pointing out the stripy fish that swam around their legs even though they made her skin creep.

After a while she left the children in the water and sat next to Carl who was asleep in the shade. She had asked him to come on holiday for some help with the kids but so far he had slept his way around most of Cuba or stared out of the car window listening to his music. But she looked at him with his long lanky body and closed eyes and realised that she was just pleased to have another adult around; someone who could help even if they didn't and someone to talk things through with, even if they never had. But what if it had been Andrew lying there? She knew she would have been irritated, annoyed and resentful. Before they had had children their relationship had been equal. But since children, somewhere out of nowhere they had evolved into a traditional couple from the 1950's. Andrew had dug deep down into his biological self and emerged as the hunter gatherer, and women's jobs, including the kids, had become her responsibility. She had moaned and criticised at first but this had got less over the years as she accepted that it was her role to do everything. And now she gained enormous satisfaction that every sentence her children uttered started with 'mummy' even if they just wanted the ketchup bottle that was nearer to Andrew than it was to her. But the transition back into her parent's generation had not been a benign process and had left her with a toxic combination of acceptance of her new role, and the remnants of expectations that he would help, which were inevitably never met. So when he wasn't around, she did everything and felt good about it. When he was there, she did everything but felt annoyed. And had he been lying on the beach asleep, whilst she watched the children over the top of her opened but unread book, she knew her resentment thermometer would have been several degrees higher than it was now with only Carl beside her.

That evening they showered and got ready for their dinner which was being laid out for them on the veranda. Their hosts were busy cooking in the kitchen and Jackie decided to ask if they wanted to join them, although this had seemed to be against normal procedure in the other places they had stayed. After much persuading they agreed and set two extra places although they refused to let Jackie help with the cooking or even carry anything through. The spread was prepared and seemed to be enough food to feed several families, with mountains of rice and black bean sauce, piles of sweet potato chips and green beans, cucumber and avocado straight from the garden. Even the chicken tasted fresh and looked like chicken used to before it was routinely pumped full of water and hormones, and was brownish rather than the yellow of the ones Jackie tried to buy in England.

'This is wonderful,' said Jackie. 'Where do you buy the food? We haven't really seen any shops yet?'

Marco and Maria described how they shared a car with their neighbours to go to a market just outside Trinidad and also explained how lucky they were to have so much land and how much of the food was home grown. They chatted for a while about their different jobs and families. Then Jackie decided it was time to unleash all the thoughts that had been building up since arriving in Cuba.

'Can I ask you some questions?' she said 'About Cuba. It's all so interesting and there's so much I don't understand.'

Her hosts looked a bit worried and braced themselves for the onslaught, saying: 'OK. But we have to be careful you know.'

So Jackie asked away.

'How do you get a house here?' she said 'Some people have wonderful houses and other don't. How does that work?' They described that most people lived in their parents' or their spouse's parents' house. If you wanted a new house you had to apply to the government when you had found some land and bought at least half the materials to buy it.

'But that could take ages. Forever in fact,' said Jackie.

Marco and Maria nodded.

'How do you get a job?' Jackie asked. 'Are jobs ever advertised?'

Marco explained that if you went to university you were put into a track for a job when you left, then this was what you did. So he became a doctor and his wife became an economist but if they had studied art they would have become painters or if they had studied tourism they would have worked for the tourist industry. If you left school without going to university the decision was just made that bit earlier.

'But what if you want to change jobs?' she asked.

'Well,' said Maria 'you have to ask your manager in the Communist party if you can and they will find you another job.'

'So if you are a painter, then that's what you do forever?' she said, thinking of Oscar sitting in the Cathedral square.

'Yes,' they said 'unless you can't anymore.'

'Like me,' said Marco, showing them his twisted hands. 'I had to leave medicine and so now we work in tourism.'

'And do you work for yourself or the government?' said Jackie. 'Are you self employed?'

'We work for ourselves but we pay tax to the government. A lot of tax,' said Maria.

'And the people in the markets? Are they self employed?' Jackie asked.

'Yes. At the moment,' they said. 'But Castro keeps changing his mind. So sometimes he allows us to have our own businesses but then he panics and claims them all back again.'

They finished their meal and the children went off to play and Jackie bombarded them with more questions. She found out about the political dissidents who had been imprisoned for trying to set up an opposition party and their wives and mothers, known as the women in white, who met every week in Havana to protest about their captivity. They told her about the men who were killed for trying to leave the country, the corruption in the Communist party with high up members having modern cars, large houses and passports also the lack of infra structure causing bad roads, poor public transport and an electricity supply that had a mind of its own. But she also found out about the role of the US. They also told her how the CIA had made numerous attempts to assassinate Castro, how the US refused to trade with them, how several Cuban political activists were held in American prisons and how consecutive US governments had been too afraid to negotiate with Castro for fear of alienating the right wing ex Cubans living in Florida.

'So what do you think should happen?' Jackie asked as the night was drawing to a close and the children were by now fast asleep.

'It's complicated,' said Marco. 'But we need a new American president to take the pressure off us. Whilst Castro feels under siege he acts as if everyone is his enemy. And we are the ones that suffer. Not the Americans, but Castro's people. The Cubans. The ones he is supposed to be protecting.'

'So it's all the fault of the US?' she asked finally.

'It was,' Maria said. 'But things could have changed if Castro had managed it all differently.'

Eight

The next day had been planned as one of the highlights of the holiday. Near Trinidad was an old sugar plantation that had been home to thousands of black slaves right up until the end of the 19th century. They had decided to have lunch there and wander around the grounds. Toby and Vicky had been enticed by the promise of seeing how sugar was produced, followed by an afternoon on the beach, and for once Carl seemed interested in what they were about to do and joined in the conversation over breakfast.

'My family comes from Jamaica,' he explained to the children. 'Way way back, they were slaves on a sugar plantation. They were brought over from Africa as part of the slave trade and sold to the plantation owners.'

'That's cool,' said Toby.

'Not really,' said Carl, which made Toby flinch as 'cool' was very much Carl's word and most things seemed to fit the 'cool' category.

'There was a television programme on when I was a child,' said Jackie 'called Roots. It was all about slavery and followed the life of one man, from being captured in Africa to living as a slave in America. Everyone watched it. It was amazing. I can still remember that his African name was

Kunte Kinte but they made him change it to try and get rid of his African identity.'

'Why didn't they fight back or run away?' asked Toby.

'They were chained up and had to wear shackles. And if they did try to get away they were beaten or even shot,' said Jackie.

'I read once that loads of them committed suicide,' said Carl 'because their life was so hard.'

'Did the English have slaves, mummy?' asked Vicky.

'Yes darling, we did. So did the Spanish, the French and the Americans. But we let ours go quite early on. Cuban slaves were some of the last to be freed. I think that's why so many Cubans are black. They are descended from the slaves who were brought here from Africa'.

'And that's why Jamaica has so many black people living there,' said Carl. 'And the US.'

'We don't have many black people in Surrey, mummy,' said Vicky. 'Did we have slaves in Surrey?'

'No, darling. All the slaves were kept abroad on colonies managed by rich land owners. There were no colonies in Surrey. No slaves. Just wives,' she laughed. Vicky didn't really get the joke.

Jackie had lived most of her life in London where she had had friends from all different ethnic groups and most of the main religions. They had moved out of London to improve her work/life balance so that she could keep her career going and pick up the kids from school, but she had found the 'whiteness' of the area shocking and had come up against prejudices that she hadn't realised existed anymore. One neighbour often told her husband that she was 'running away with a black man' when she was going to be late, making Jackie flinch. And this same husband had once said, 'Well let's be honest we all live in Surrey to get away from black people,' which had sent Jackie into a paroxysm of justifications, explanations and defensiveness, all of which had fallen on deaf ears. But the move had meant that her children were now having a very different cultural life from the one she had had and she was determined that Cuba would add to their understanding that there were many more types of people in the world than the white ones they mixed with in Surrey.

After breakfast they headed off to the plantation. It wasn't far and they were quickly paying a very friendly man to stop their tyres being taken by the tyre thieves, who were never anywhere to be seen, but seemed to keep a lot of parking attendants in work. This man was very pleased to be paid but had no arms and Jackie did

briefly wonder what he would do if the thieves
appeared, but she dismissed the thought as
inappropriate. They turned a corner to walk to the
house and were instantly surrounded by women
thrusting jewellery at them by the handfuls. There
were strings of necklaces all tied together and
clusters of bracelets all beautifully crafted out of
seeds, fruit stones and what looked like coloured
sweet corn and Jackie wanted to think about
buying some but the women's frenzy made it hard
to focus. One was heavily pregnant and kept
pointing to her bump saying: 'For baby. Please, for
baby.' One was pressing the necklaces to her
chest, whilst saying: 'You have shampoo, sun
cream?' and another grabbed hold of Toby saying:
'My son, like yours. Buy jewellery please.' She tried
to talk to each of them, ask questions and be
polite but in the end she just bought the same
bundles of the same items from each of them,
handed out far too much money for what she had
and scurried off.

'God! That was hard work,' she said to Carl as
they walked up the steps to the house. 'What am I
going to do with all these? Do you want six of the
same bracelet? They would look lovely with six of
the same necklace.'

The plantation was in the middle of a vast
plain covered with trees, bushes and yellow soil
and at one end was a grand mansion with stone
steps leading up to a huge double wooden door,

bright white plastered walls and an overhanging roof with blue beams. They paid their entrance fee and stood in a wide central hallway with high ceilings, brass ceiling fans and cool marble flooring and Jackie half expected Rhett Butler to arrive at any time or Vivienne Leigh to swan down the staircase. And around the walls were paintings of slaves. There were black men holding their shackles, black women cutting the sugar beet and slaves in the fields in the heat working while their masters looked on. And if you wanted, you could buy wooden carvings of slaves with wooden chains preventing them from running away. Jackie found it quite shocking and Carl even took his earphones out whilst he was looking around.

'It's dreadful to think that people were treated like this,' he said.

'What people do to each other is horrible.'

'They're like animals,' said Toby. 'All chained up.'

'Those chains look really heavy,' said Vicky. 'And that sun. It all looks so hard.'

'I know, darlings. It's horrible,' said Jackie. 'But at least they were freed. We don't do this anymore. Not here, anyway.'

They stood in silence for a while looking at the sculptures and the paintings and then decided to have a drink in the café before heading out into the plantation itself. The café was at the back of the mansion and they sat outside under the roof on a balcony overlooking the fields and woods below. There were chickens and pigs in the yard and in the distance they could see an enormous tower looking out over the plantation. Vicky needed to go to the toilet as soon as their drinks arrived and Jackie got up to take her. Just outside the toilet was a young woman sitting at a table selling toilet paper, which had become a familiar sight on their holiday. Jackie resented having to pay for something so basic, when they were already paying for their drinks and the entrance fee, and often just brought her own, but today she paid the woman some change from her pocket.

'Are you on holiday?' asked the woman.

'Yes,' said Jackie. 'We're from England. We've been here a week and are staying just outside Trinidad.'

'I have a daughter. She is the same age as yours,' the woman said pointing at Vicky.

'Oh! Yes, she's seven,' said Jackie and hurried into the toilet with memories of the frenzy from the women outside.

When they came out the woman was still there and smiled at them. She looked around her and then unobtrusively gave them a piece of toilet paper with her name and address on it.

'Can you send me some things for my daughter, please?' she said. 'Shoes, clothes, anything you have.'

Jackie looked at her properly now. She had a very open face with smiling eyes. She seemed calmer than the women outside and Jackie no longer felt the need to run away.

'What is your daughter called?' she asked.

The woman said her daughter's name was Lola and she lived with her family on the plantation. She also described how she had studied for three years at a university and had then completed an extra year for a diploma in tourism. This was her tourism job.

'Selling toilet paper?' asked Jackie, shocked.

The woman nodded and Jackie took the piece of paper back with her to the table to tell Carl what the woman had said.

'God that's terrible,' said Carl. 'I don't have a degree but even I wouldn't sell toilet paper. Why don't they use toilet roll holders like everyone else. It's degrading doing that for a living.'

'I guess that's how they have no unemployment. Everybody has a job, even if it's doing something like that,' said Jackie. 'When we were in China they had one person to take your coat, one to see you to your seat and one to give you your meal.'

'And one to gob on the floor,' said Toby who had heard her parents tell the story of their trip to China loads of times, with tales of people clearing their throat and noses wherever they felt like it.

'But maybe they don't mind it here,' said Jackie. 'Maybe we expect too much from our jobs.' But she knew that if she looked over at the woman sitting at her little table she wouldn't be convinced by what she was saying.

After their drinks they waved good bye to the woman at the toilets and headed off to explore. Their first stop was the lookout tower, made from a wooden frame filled in with white plaster with about five blocks of steps winding their way up to the very top and open arched platforms to break the climb at every stage. The pointed summit had large openings on all four sides and it didn't take much to imagine the guards standing up there with their guns aimed at anyone attempting to make their bid for freedom. Carl set off up the stairs first and bounded his way to the first stage followed by the children, with Jackie at the end with the optimistic plan to catch anyone who fell. The climb was steep and it was hot and sticky and by the time they got near the top Jackie was pushing Vicky up step by step from behind whilst Toby and Carl looked down on them red faced and bright eyed. But the view from the top was worth it. Stretching beneath them were acres of yellow fields each edged by hedges with some still showing the strips of sugar cane plants lined up from end to end. There were rich green woods in the distance and along the path nearer to the foot of the tower were clusters of metal and wooden shacks some joined together in terrace-like rows and others just randomly dotted around. All looked uninhabited - memories of a time long past, with weeds winding over them, reclaiming them back into nature.

'Look darlings,' said Jackie 'that must have been where the slaves used to live; in those buildings down there.'

'It looks like that film we saw mummy, when they dug a tunnel and escaped from the camp,' said Vicky.

'It does. You're right,' said Jackie 'but I don't think anyone ever escaped from here.'

They stayed at the top where a breeze cooled their hot faces and chatted about what it must have been like to be a slave and taken to work somewhere like Cuba. Toby and Vicky were particularly shocked at the thought of being forced to leave your family and live in a foreign country, which Jackie found quite satisfying as she had always harboured a fear that her children would live far away when they grew up. Toby was also shocked that slaves worked for nothing; and Carl enjoyed knowing about something and being able to tell them details about his own family's history. After a while they headed slowly down the steps which seemed more frightening than on the way up and Jackie made sure Carl was at the front this time in case of any accidents. As they approached the final block of steps they saw the woman from the toilets beaming up at them holding the hand of her little girl who was exactly the same height as Vicky and had the look of child who was at exactly the same stage.

'This is Lola,' she said as they reached the bottom. 'I'm Olivia.'

Jackie and the children went over and said hello to them both and Vicky and Lola stood next to each other looking each other up and down.

'Would you like me to show you around?' said Olivia. 'You can see where the sugar is grown. I have some you can try if you like.'

So they followed Olivia back to her house. They found a small dusty overgrown path that ran from the foot of the tower and wound its way through some of the shacks they had seen earlier. By now the sun was high in the sky and the air was getting thick with the heat and the dusty ground brushed up with every step. They went past an old woman carrying a bucket of water and an old man sitting on a step outside one of the metal shacks, with a row of the reversible handmade dolls in the glassless window, just in case someone should want to buy one. Some of the buildings looked deserted, even close up, but many had signs of life with flowery curtains hanging from the windows or wooden chairs outside. After a few minutes Olivia turned off the path and took them into the front yard of one of the more run-down looking shacks. The grass was long, littered with half buried old tyres, buckets and broken planks of wood. Lola ran ahead and stood by the doorway as they went in.

It took a moment for their eyes to adjust to the darkness inside, but as they did Olivia asked them to sit down on one of the four rocking chairs laid out in a square in each of the corners of a tiny room. The walls were made of horizontal strips of wood with the light gaping through each of the cracks. The ceiling was low and the walls were bare and grey, apart from a photograph of Lola that was mounted in a frame and took pride of place. The room was divided from the back section by a spindly set of shelves on which were two plastic dolls, some brightly coloured plastic cups and plates and a box of bricks. Beyond the shelves there was what looked like the remnants of a kitchen with an old broken sink half hanging from one of the walls, but there was no sign of anywhere to cook or any water supply. Before sitting down Jackie had a quick look out of the back doorway which didn't have a door and saw a broken toilet in a small shed and a over grown back yard littered with parts of the house that were broken and no longer of any use. Three young women and an older woman emerged from the next room to welcome them and through the doorway she could see rows of mattresses, blankets and pillows.

'My mother and my sisters,' said Olivia. 'All women here. No men,' she laughed. 'I'll get the sugar cane.'

Olivia went through the back door and reappeared carrying a long stick higher than the room and a sharp knife. They all followed her out to the front yard and Carl helped her to break the cane into pieces and slice back the outside to reveal the moist sugary granules inside. The children licked it and were amazed that it tasted like sugar and that it wasn't in small paper packets, while Lola watched, looking amazed that they were amazed.

'It's like sweets, mummy,' said Vicky.

'Can we keep it? I'm going to take some into school,' said Toby.

Jackie and Carl went back inside to leave the children to eat their sugar and sat down with the two sisters who were now rocking in their chairs, busy making two beautiful white embroidered cloths that were draped across their knees.

'So how long have you lived here?' asked Jackie.

'My family have always lived here,' said Olivia. 'Ever since they arrived in Cuba'

'Wow!' said Carl 'Your family used to be slaves here? Mine were slaves as well, but in Jamaica.'

'So you live in Jamaica now?' asked Olivia.

'Oh no. I live in England. Although I still have some family there. I haven't been to Jamaica, though,' said Carl.

'And is it just you women, then?' asked Jackie.

'Yes,' said Olivia. 'My father died and Lola's father lives in Trinidad with his family. I bring her up on my own. That's why I asked for help. It's very difficult. I don't get paid much and my job here will end soon'.

'Mummy,' said Vicky coming in from the garden 'can we go to the beach, and can Lola come with us?'

'That would be nice but I expect they have other things to do,' said Jackie.

'Do you?' asked Carl. 'Why don't you come with us? The kids would love it.'

'In your car?' asked Olivia 'but how would I get back?'

'Don't worry,' said Carl 'Jackie can bring you back. Can't you Jackie?'

So it was agreed. And after Olivia quickly changed out of her work clothes they piled into the car and headed back to their fishing village. Lola sat on her mother's knee chattering excitedly in Spanish to anyone who would listen, whilst Toby and Vicky giggled as she seemed completely unconcerned that they couldn't understand anything she was saying.

The beach was quite quiet for once and Jackie organised some bread and cheese from their house as they sat under a tree to eat their lunch.

'OK!' said Carl jumping up. 'Who's coming into the sea?'

Toby and Vicky pulled Lola to her feet and rushed off after Carl.

'I'd better come as well,' said Olivia. 'She can't swim.'

Jackie sat back against the tree, stretched out her legs and took a drink of her icy beer as the others ran off down to the brown water which hadn't moved since the day before.

'Bliss!' she said out loud. 'This is bliss.'

She was still ploughing her way through Castro's autobiography and now she got it out to see him in his green army combats looking as honest and moral as ever. But somehow her enthusiasm for it was starting to wane. Castro was describing how poor Cuba had been before the revolution, yet she had seen plenty of poverty on her travels. There were glorious tales of Castro meeting numerous international leaders with pictures of him in Russia, South America and the US, yet the people she had met weren't allowed to leave the country. And there were endless stories of how Castro had been outspoken against repression, had fought for freedom and had headed up many opposition groups in his youth and yet the people she had talked to were frightened to speak their mind. He even revelled in his observation that the current students in Cuba didn't need ever to demonstrate as they were content with the political regime, which made Jackie angry as she thought of her own political times as a student under a much less controlling regime in England. And there was also the issue of race. At the centre of the book was a picture of Nelson Mandela and Castro embracing - best of friends as Castro had helped release him from prison. Mandela was one of her heroes. She had been on many anti apartheid demonstrations in her life and had petitioned for their campus residence to be renamed 'Mandela house'. But Cuba was beginning to make her feel like a white colonial with privileges not available to the black Cubans. She had different money to the Cubans, could go on different beaches, drink in different restaurants, watch international television and leave the country whenever she wanted. And here was Olivia living in an old slave shack, on the same plantation as her ancestors, selling toilet paper to the white tourists, who were visiting to see just how badly people had been treated in the past. She put the thick tome down and lay back to watch the peace of the sea.

Nine

'Mummy, can Lola have dinner with us?' said Vicky. 'Please, mummy.'

'I'm sure they need to get home,' said Jackie 'Their family will be expecting them. And we can't ask Marco and Maria to cook for two extra.'

'We could eat somewhere else,' said Carl. 'What about a night out in Trinidad?'

They had all come back to the house to shower after a hot afternoon on the beach and Vicky and Lola had been doing some colouring whilst Carl and Olivia had been sitting on the veranda overlooking the sea.

'It says in this book they have dancing in the square for the locals. We could eat and then watch the dancing. You like salsa, Jackie, don't you? I believe you do some good moves,' said Carl grinning at her.

'And you're suddenly all lively,' said Jackie grinning back. 'Do you fancy coming out with us tonight, Olivia, then I could run you back home later on?'

With a face that couldn't physically smile any harder, Olivia hugged Jackie and told Lola, who then hugged everyone one by one, squealing in very fast high pitch Spanish.

Without hesitation, Vicky lent Lola one of her favourite skirts and tops. Olivia, who had only come in her beach wear, borrowed Jackie's red dress and a Cuban necklace which looked stunning on her and she walked tall around the veranda for everyone to see.

'You look beautiful,' said Jackie. 'I wish it looked that good on me.'

'It does mummy,' said Vicky. 'You're beautiful too.'

'What do you think Carl?' asked Jackie smiling.

But Carl just grinned back and went off to get washed and ready.

The evening was getting cooler by the time they reached Trinidad and the sky was almost black, although the fluorescent strip lights from the porches lit the streets. They parked the car, paid a man - with arms this time - to watch it, and then found a restaurant with doors opening onto the street and a resident band of four men playing music to the guests.

'Olivia,' said Jackie as they sat down. 'Why are there so many people with limbs missing? I seem to have a seen a lot of people without legs or arms.'

Jackie had a personal issue with missing limbs, as a good friend had had a flying accident a few years before and had lost his leg. It had been a dreadful time of operations, skin grafts and strong drugs but in the end they had decided to amputate and it had been shocking to see him for the first time with only one foot sticking out from under the sheets. But after a short period of drinking too much to numb the horrible pain from the leg that was no longer there he had adapted to his prosthetic limb which enabled him to walk and even cycle as well as anyone. And now he lived a normal life and no one would ever know except that one shoe was always shinier than the other. But he had been left with two pet hates. The first was being told of those who had run marathons or crossed deserts with artificial limbs. 'But I never wanted to cross a dessert so don't see why I have to now,' he would say. The second was people he saw as going for the sympathy vote and occasionally he would go up to someone in the street with a limb missing and berate them for not using their prosthesis, whilst lifting his trouser leg to show them his.

'It's from the war, I think,' said Olivia. 'Castro sent us to fight in Angola and we lost 10,000 men and many more were injured'

'What do you think of Castro?' asked Jackie.

Olivia placed her hand across her heart and said: 'He's my father. My saviour. He's a wonderful man.'

'Why do you think that?' asked Carl.

'He saved this country. People working the fields were poor. They couldn't read or write. They got sick. Now we have jobs. We have doctors. And I've been to university. I have studied for four years. My family is proud of me. That would never have happened without Castro.'

'But your life seems hard,' said Carl.

'It is hard,' she said. 'But I have Lola and my family. My role is to give Lola a good start in life. And that makes me happy.'

'I don't really know what my role is,' said Carl quietly, looking at Olivia. 'You're lucky.'

'I am. In a way,' she said.

They ordered lobster as a treat, which came with piles of rice and vegetables and chicken for the children, who seemed more interested in the lobster once it arrived, with its crackers for breaking open the claws and bright red eyes. Olivia had had neither wine nor lobster before and Lola was so excited about being in a restaurant that their table was soon buzzing with laughter and chat. Toby and Vicky told their stories of climbing the mountain, having a lizard hanging off their ear and enormous black spiders, Jackie gave a censored description of the music on the veranda and her dance with the Mexican, and Olivia offered tales of her life as a student in

Havana and encounters with different tourists at the plantation. Even Carl, who hadn't seemed to notice much of their holiday until now, entertained them all with how he could have changed the tyre on the motorway and how the crocodiles kept trying to get at them through the fence. And every now and again they would stop to listen to the band, who played their drums and guitars and sang their rhythmical music.

Then it was time to walk up to the square and watch the dancing.

By now the children were getting weary and Carl carried Lola on his shoulders whilst Jackie and Olivia coaxed Toby and Vicky up the street trying to make staying up late into the treat it always seemed to be when they were expected to be in bed at a reasonable time.

'But I'm tired,' said Toby. 'I want to go to bed.'

'My legs won't walk any further,' said Vicky.

But when they saw where they were heading - as ever - energy was dredged out of nowhere. The square was at the top of the town flanked by the grand buildings of the museum and the town hall with their pillars, large windows and sandstone walls which towered over the rest of Trinidad's houses. It was formally laid out with low brick walls, small hedges and lamps around the outside and in the middle a dried up fountain with a green statue that must one day have poured out water into the well below. And wherever you looked were young men and women out for the evening sitting on every bench, every wall and every spare knee of everyone else. The air was filled with the noise of fun and flirting and people were softly strumming their guitars or stroking their drums. Then as they wandered over to sit in a small space between the masses, the drumming, guitars and clapping started up in unison and people paired up effortlessly to dance. Men and women seemed to choose each other without the anxiety or hesitation that Jackie remembered from her youth and they all knew every song and every set of moves that went with it. The men spun the women and the women were happy to be spun. The feet moved, the arms held arms and the hips brushed other hips as eyes locked into eyes. The music had a rhythm that made time lose itself and they all sat watching as the evening cooled with Toby and Vicky lounging across Jackie's knee and Lola strewn across Olivia and Carl. At various times men of all ages would come across to ask Jackie and Olivia to dance but after their day in the heat, sitting and watching as the children drifted off to sleep was all they wanted to do.

....

Jackie and the kids spent the next few days on the beach. Most beaches in much of the world are designed to be family friendly. They are littered with shops selling brightly coloured plastic, moulded into anything relating to sand and sea, with ice cream kiosks and endless cafes to buy drinks and snacks. There is very little need to bring anything from home and every child's whim can be catered for as soon as the whim arises. Their beach in Cuba had none of these luxuries but was teeming with families and none of what was not there seemed to matter. Occasionally men wearing large straw hats and shorts would wander past selling fruit or homemade bags of popcorn or roasted nuts and a man set up his stall one morning under a tree selling a few inflatables for kids. When they wanted a drink the kids wandered back to the house and seemed to entertain themselves for hours jumping off the rock that Jackie now allowed them to venture out to. They saw parents with their children standing in waist deep water chatting under umbrellas or catching them as they leapt off the rocks. .They watched teenagers hanging out in groups under the trees wearing very little, playing guitars and singing quietly. Toby and the local boys waded in the shallows with their home-made lines, hooks and buckets staring for hours into the water and squealing as they pulled out a stripy or silver swordfish with long pointed nose. And when Olivia and Lola came to visit, the girls spent ages bobbing around in the water in their new rubber rings. The smell was one of salt and bodies; the sound was of gentle talk and warmth and the sky was always and unrelentingly blue. And from the beach Jackie watched as a version of Carl she had never seen before raced the kids, threw them in the air, splashed them and taught Lola and Olivia how to swim.

Carl. There are many black men in South London who stay on at school, go to college, have careers and stay out of trouble with the police. Then there is the stereotype of the South London black man. He is the man who wears a hoody, has trousers held on below his bottom by the tightest of belts and hangs out with his mates during the day. And he is the one who spends more time than any South London white man being stopped by the police just for driving his car, questioned by the police for just being out and about and if the spiral is allowed to continue ends up feeling picked on, paranoid and that the law is not on his side. Carl's mum was a friend of a friend of Jackie and she felt that Carl was on the cusp of that stereotype and at the top of that spiral. He had stayed on at school and passed most of his exams. He had even gone to college, but in the last year or so he had lost his focus. He was average at most things but felt he had no natural talent to show him the way forward. He'd had a few jobs but none had really worked out and then he was drifting. And although many men of his age drift for a while and it all turns out for the best, his mum didn't like his new friends and worried about his new aimless life so had sent him off to Surrey to give him time out to find his way. That was six months ago and since then he had either slept so much he seemed to be hibernating, listened to music, or just been around with the kids eating and beating them at games.

'Jackie,' he said coming over from the sea. 'Jackie. Can I ask you something?'

'Of course. Fire away.'

He sat down next to her looking more tentative than usual and took his sunglasses off.

'Jackie,' he said. 'Olivia has no money.'

'I know Carl. She has a hard life.'

'She has never had a holiday,' he said.

'I'm not surprised.'

'Nor has Lola.'

Jackie looked at him as he continued.

'She has never stayed in a hotel,' he said.

They both paused for a moment, looking back out to sea.

'Would you like her to come back to Havana with us?' said Jackie. 'I was thinking we could just about squeeze them in the car and I thought you might like that.'

Carl broke out into a smile of relief at not having to actually ask, topped up with an added smile of pure pleasure.

'I fancy a couple of nights in a posh hotel. It would be good for all of us.'

'Thanks Jackie,' he said, putting his arm around her for the first time ever. 'You're a star. A complete star.'

'I try to be. But I don't always manage it,' she said. 'Ask Andrew.'

Ten

Two days later they left Trinidad to head back to Havana for the final stage of their trip. Olivia and Lola squeezed into the back with the kids and the car was beginning to look more Cuban with arms, legs and luggage everywhere. The car was buzzing with chat for the first part of the journey as they imagined what the hotel would be like, listing every possible form of luxury they could indulge in. The plan was to stay there for two nights as Olivia needed to get back to work, but it looked as though those two days were going to be crammed full of swimming, eating, dancing, having Jacuzzis, and playing tennis. Toby and Vicky wanted to have a sauna, although this seemed a bit bizarre given that it was so hot all the time. But after a while the car went quiet and the children, read while Carl and Olivia stared out of the window.

Jackie watched as Cuban motorway life passed by and felt less surprised now by the cows and onion sellers at the side of the road or the occasional person who ran across the central barrier. And she used the peace in the car to think. It was just over a week since they had left home but Andrew and her life in Surrey seemed very distant. Her routines of the daily school run with its stresses of getting kids dressed, fed and out of the house on time, the choices about what to feed

111

everyone and the hectic schedule of after-school clubs, friends for tea and trips to the park all wrapped around a full time job seemed like a world belonging to a different person in a different place. And Andrew. They had a good life spending nice days in interesting places, and at times in Cuba she had missed his conversation and rational mind. But she hadn't missed the tension and the feeling of being sensitised to someone's every mood and every move. It felt nice to be always happy; to be the better version of herself, who could be warm and calm, not cool and irritated. And it made her proud of herself that she could be so self sufficient; the adult who was managing everything.

So as they drove closer to Havana, thoughts and images of Oscar crept into her head. She could picture flashes of him laughing, the way his hips moved when he danced and his eyes as they held onto her stare. She replayed their time together in the cathedral square watching Cuban life, having dinner listening to the band and on the beach under the straw umbrella. She played the tape forward to a place not yet visited - of bodies, thighs and mouths. And she put her foot down to speed up their journey.

They arrived back in Havana and managed to find their way to the Hotel National, which was at the bottom of a wide boulevard high up on a hill overlooking the sea. The guidebook gave lists of singers, politicians and royalty who had stayed there and as they were allowed under the barrier and drove up the steep winding road Jackie felt the excitement of extravagance that she didn't often allow herself. They parked the car in the guarded car park without any threat of tyre thieves this time and walked down the steps to the entrance hall.

From outside the hotel was impressive. It was a like America's own White House but much higher and with rows of palm trees lining its driveway. It had white walls and layers upon layers of windows and balconies reaching their way up to the two towers at the top which looked out to sea. There was a vast circular fountain at its foot and a grassy bank heading down to the sea road. But from the inside it was even more opulent. They walked through the large revolving doors into a vast tunnel-like entrance hall and found a world of style and class that none of them had seen before. The floors were paved in marble, the ceiling was dizzyingly high and long, and seemingly never-ending walls were lined with dark mahogany and broken up by archways leading into shops and cafés. There were clusters of brown leather sofas for people to rest drink or talk; dark wooden tables for newspapers and books; and wooden stands for hats and coats. Then on one side of this long dark hall were arched stained glass windows leading out onto the veranda where people sat on white wicker chairs watching the wild fowl elegantly wander around the sloped gardens below.

Jackie got the price list from the reception desk behind large wooden shutters and they sat down on some sofas to work out what they wanted to do. They could see signs in gold writing showing the way to swimming pools, restaurants and bars and dark wooden display cases detailing the times of the hotel's entertainment with pictures of elaborate dancers in gaudy costumes, synchronised swimmers in their flowery caps and musicians dressed in evening wear. And people wearing their smart clothes could be seen pulling their designer luggage or waiting for their private taxi. This was an international hotel and everyone was from everywhere in the world other than Cuba.

'This is wonderful,' said Olivia. 'I've heard about this place but I never thought I would get here.'

'It's definitely posh,' said Carl.

'It's beautiful,' said Jackie, then paused leaving a silence hanging.

'What?' said Carl 'I can hear a "but" coming. Is it too expensive?'

The prices were much higher than anything they had paid so far, but compared to a top hotel in England they were quite manageable and Jackie had always planned to spend some of the holiday in luxury. She wanted to offer everyone a night to remember and she realised that Olivia would never be able to afford somewhere like this without her. But she felt uncomfortable. Since being in Cuba she had seen a lot of poverty and the difference between those with and those without seemed huge. Some people had passports, some didn't. Some had cars and some crammed themselves into a cattle truck. Some lived in wooden shacks, some had spare rooms for tourists and some, she guessed, probably had greater luxury than she had come across. And those who seemed to have the most were always part of the regime. This was a state-owned hotel. And all the people she could see now looked nothing like any of the people she had met on the rest of their trip.

'I just feel uncomfortable. That's all,' she said quietly. 'This is not really why I came to Cuba.'

'But why? It's wonderful here. This is part of our history. Look at everything you can do. This is Cuba at its best,' said Olivia.

'But all the money. It will all go to the Communist party. To Castro,' said Jackie 'The contrast. Think of where you live and what you have.'

'But Castro is like my father. He is my saviour,' she said, placing her hand across her heart as she had done before.

'It just feels wrong,' said Jackie.

'But we could eat wonderful food, swim in that beautiful pool and do things I've always dreamt of doing,' said Olivia.

'And give all that money to people who already seem to have more than they should,' said Jackie.

'It's not their money. It's our money,' said Olivia 'This is Communism. We are all in it together.'

There was a long pause between them and they both looked down. This was a clash of two completely different worlds that would probably never be resolved. How could someone who had so little ever understand why someone who could have everything didn't want it. Jackie felt confused and unsure of what to do. She knew that it would be wonderful for Olivia to have the chance to stay somewhere like this but she wasn't sure she could bring herself to give a large amount of money to a regime she was now uncertain about.

'It's your money, Jackie,' said Carl after a while. 'We could always go back and stay with Ernesto again. It was nice there. I'm not sure

Castro and his lot should have even more of our money if they don't have to.'

Olivia looked between him and Jackie, and was starting to look frantic. 'Carl,' she said 'I thought you wanted to be here. I thought we would have fun together.'

'I did,' he said 'I do. But you have to admit it does feel a bit strange.'

'This isn't strange. It's wonderful,' she said.

'But it is a bit odd. All this money,' he said.

'Carl. You have no idea about anything. Don't just copy her. Think for yourself.'

'I do think for myself. It's you that doesn't,' he snapped. The air went quiet.

'I've always thought for myself,' she said softly 'always done everything for myself.'

Olivia got up and pulled Lola to her feet.

'I think we should go now,' she said. 'I need my bags from the car'.

They all stood up talking over each other with everyone feeling annoyed with everyone else that the day wasn't turning out as they had planned. The kids were pleading with Olivia to stay, Olivia was cross with Carl, Carl was trying to justify what he had said but was making the situation worse and Jackie was thinking that perhaps she had overreacted and made a mistake.

Then out of nowhere two policemen appeared. They were wearing tight green uniforms and had guns and large wooden sticks attached to their belts.

'Please come with us,' one said. 'We would like to talk with you.'

Then, despite Lola crying, Carl getting angry and Jackie's attempts to discuss, negotiate and argue, a few minutes later Carl and Olivia were led out of the building. And Jackie was left in the Hotel National in the middle of Cuba alone with three children, one of whom wasn't even hers.

Eleven

Carl's story

I've been sitting in this room on my own for about ten minutes now. They took us to a car outside the hotel and drove through the most run-down parts of Havana until we reached the police station. One of the guys seemed to enjoy smirking over his shoulder trying to scare us, then kept muttering in quick quiet Spanish to his friend. Olivia didn't say much but held my hand tightly the whole way. She seemed really worried, poor thing. We passed all of Cuban life along the way and the streets were busy with people doing whatever it is they do here but no one seemed to notice either us or the police car. I felt like the conspicuous tourist who had been wrongly arrested but I guess two black people in the back of a police car is nothing new here as well as everywhere else I have ever lived.

It's a small square room and the walls are white, just like the interview rooms in England really, but a bit scruffier with patches of damp and peeling paint everywhere. And I'm allowed to smoke which would be great, except I don't anymore and don't want to start again now. I think Olivia is in the room next door but I can't hear anything. They left me here saying they were going to speak to her first and since then it's all been quiet. I have no idea what they think we have done. Maybe they think we've stolen something from the hotel. I don't know. Perhaps someone called them and thought we looked suspicious. Not wearing the right clothes. Not carrying the right bags. Maybe we were just making too much noise. We shouldn't have argued. It was silly. Jackie had a point, though I think she would have changed her mind after a while. I know she fancied some luxury as much as the rest of us did. And she's been so good to me I felt I should give her some support. But then I guess that really upset Olivia. God! It's hard trying to keep everyone happy.

I'm still here, alone and it must be about half an hour since they left. I thought I heard a noise next door but then it went quiet. It's really creepy. Sitting here. Waiting. Listening to the creaking and wondering what's going on. I don't know what their rules are here. Can they just keep us locked up? I don't know what their prisons are like. Maybe they can just do whatever they like. I was really starting to enjoy the holiday. But I guess I'll be out soon. It's been an hour now and I still haven't seen anyone. I've had my fair share of trouble with the police over the past few years in London but it's never been like this. I've always known what they think I've done even if I haven't done it. Usually it's been the car I'm driving or the bike I'm on. 'Is this yours?' they say and want to see every document they can think of. Once they wanted to know whose jacket I was wearing. The problem is that it never is my car or my bike. And that wasn't even my jacket, I'd borrowed it off a friend. So then it all looks suspicious and they take me in to question. But at least they talk to me. They ask questions. I know what I'm doing there. This silence is horrible. Maybe they have just forgotten that they brought both of us in. Maybe they want to make me scared. Maybe they are going to put on the speakers so I can hear her confess to whatever it is we are supposed to have done like they do in the films. Well I suppose I am scared. My leg keeps shaking and I can feel my heart through my shirt.

Still no sign of anyone and it's been nearly two hours. I've tried banging on the door but no one comes. I've called and I've shouted but nothing happens. I'm hot now. My leg won't stop moving. Every now and again it just twitches all on its own. I don't like being on my own. When I was little, my mum sometimes left me. Not for long. But she needed to go to the shops just to get bread or milk or something. And after my Dad had left it was just the two of us so she didn't have much choice. It was either that or no breakfast in the morning. I'd tell her I'd be fine and I really thought I would be but it always seemed to last too long. I'd watch TV, play on the computer, read my book then after a while I'd just sit by the window waiting. When she got back I'd try not to look too relieved so she didn't feel guilty but I'd always follow her around for the rest of the evening, checking that she was still there.

They've just gone. Only stayed for a few minutes but at least I've seen someone. I thought I was going mad. I was getting all fidgety. I was really sweating. They say they'll be back in a few minutes to ask me some questions about Olivia. God knows what they want to know. I hardly know her really. I hope she's OK. They must have been in with her for ages. I like her. She's really nice, different. Most of the women I know can be great fun at times but they moan a lot. Their jobs, their flats, their families; they always seem so cross about things. And they think being cross is funny. But it's not. And they have so much. But Olivia isn't like that. She's warm and she smiles and laughs and gets on with it all. And she hardly has anything. That's impressive; to be so upbeat even when her life seems so hard.

My mum was a bit like that. Being on her own with me, but just getting on with it. Actually, I think I probably moan quite a lot as well now. I didn't used to. I used to have a great time. Great friends, the teachers were OK at school and my mum was always on my side. Whatever I did she always told me I was special and that I was going to have a good life. I worked hard. I used to love doing well in tests and telling her. I knew she would squeal and smother me. Wrapping me up in her arms. I can remember being chosen to be the lead in the school play once and she was as excited as I was. She made my costume, helped me learn my lines and came to every performance. That year I wanted to be an actor. The next year when my poem went on the classroom wall I wanted to be a writer. I don't know what went wrong really. I just lost it all somewhere along the line. Now I don't know what I want to be when I grow up and I am grown up.

They have now gone and at last I know what this is all about as I have just spent the last hour answering question after question about politics; who I voted for in England? What I thought of Cuba? What I thought of Castro? and then they wanted to know what Olivia thought of Castro. Did she talk about the government? What did she say? Was she ever critical of the government? Did I ask her questions about living in Cuba? I glossed over what I think about Castro but the rest was easy. I didn't need to lie. 'She says he is like her father' I said 'she says he is her saviour.'

They gave me a bit of a break but were back again. But this time they moved onto Olivia. How did I meet her? Where were we? What was she doing? What do I do in England? What am I doing here? Why did Olivia come back to Havana with me? Is she my girlfriend? Was I going to share a room with her in the hotel? Then they asked about Lola. Did I know her father? Was I her father? Who were Jackie's kids? Was I their father? Where was Andrew? Why hadn't he come to Cuba? It was exhausting and they were persistent but I never lied I just told it to them straight. I have no job. I have no money. Jackie paid for the holiday. Olivia is just a friend. She is not my girlfriend. I have no girlfriend. Lola is not my child. I have no children. That's all there is to it.

And now the coffee has gone cold as I stare at the wall. Not much of a life when you look at it like that.

Twelve

Olivia's story

I feel so upset. My hands are sticky and I feel
sick. The journey here was horrible. The police
ignored us and just chatted to each other as if we
weren't there. Carl ignored me and didn't say
anything and people kept staring at us through the
window. It was horrible. I wish I'd never come to
Havana. I wish I'd stayed at home. I
thought everything was going so well. Jackie had
been lovely to me and Carl was such fun and then
it all went wrong. Jackie suddenly went
all precious about everything and Carl is so weak.
He just backed her up and took her side. But then
I guess she was paying for everything. But he
could have stood up for me. Or at least he could
have kept quiet. That's why I'm on my own. It's
easier being on your own. You don't get let down.

They have just been back and brought me a
coffee. They say they are asking Carl a few
questions and then will come back. I wish I knew
what this was all about. I had a friend at college
who was interviewed by the police for ages once.
She had met a German tourist. She said it went on
forever. But nothing really happened afterwards.
Mind you I also know quite a few people who
have married tourists and left the country so you

can't blame them really for talking to us. If we all left, there would be no one left to keep the country going.

I think the past hour has been the worst hour of my life. They sat me down in this chair and then just asked me question after question. I have always loved Cuba, loved my country and been proud of having Castro as our leader. But they didn't seem to believe me. 'What did I tell Carl about Cuba?'; 'Did I mind my job at the plantation?'; 'Did I like living there with my family?'; 'What did Carl think of my house?'; 'Did I want to go to England?' On and on they went and I told them the same story over and over. 'I love my country. I am proud to be Cuban. Castro is my saviour.' One guy kept smirking at me as if I was stupid. Maybe some people want to live somewhere else. But Cuba is a beautiful country. It's never cold, it's green and we have enough food to go around. Things are so much better than they used to be. And that's all because of the regime. I have a good life. I have my family near me and I have Lola. She makes it all right somehow. It just adds up. I heard of someone who won a lottery once and the prize was a passport and a flight to Miami. They were so excited. I saw it on the TV and they kept jumping up and down and hugging everyone. I've never wanted to live anywhere else really. They had family in the States so that's probably why they wanted to go there. But my family are all here. We look after each other.

They came back again. But this time they asked about Carl. 'How did we meet?', 'Was he my boyfriend?', 'Did I want him to be my boyfriend?', 'Who was Lola's father?' Over and over they asked. I told them that Lola's father lived in Cienfuegos. He is a lovely man and was good to me but had no intention of ever leaving his wife. And I didn't really want him to. He was too old and in the long term it would never have worked out. I cope on my own and he helps out when he can with money and clothes and things. I miss having someone around sometimes. But I have my family.

I've been on my own now for nearly an hour. I keep hearing noises from next door. It must be Carl. It's not shouting but it sounds a bit angry and I heard the table being banged a couple of times. I hope he's alright. He's got nothing to hide. He's done nothing wrong. I also miss having fun. Carl is fun. He makes me laugh. He's always so lively and joins in with the kids. He's a big kid himself really. But in a nice way. He's also quite sexy. Maybe he was right about the hotel. It was Jackie's money and she could have spent it on more important things. But that hotel was so beautiful. I would have loved to stay there. Only one night would have been great. I wonder what the rooms are like. The swimming pool looked beautiful. Carl could have taught me to swim. And that dining room in the photograph looked amazing. Lola would have loved it.

They came back again but not for long this time. They said Carl had told them that I was very loyal to the regime and that I was obviously a good citizen of Cuba. They also said that Carl was obviously not my boyfriend and didn't intend to be. They are going to take us back to the hotel soon. 'To your separate rooms' they said and smirked.

My coffee has gone cold and I no longer feel sick. I just feel flat. Right now it would be nice to have someone to look after me.

Thirteen

Jackie sat back down on the sofa as the kids climbed over her, all crying and all wanting more of her than they could get. Everyone seemed to be walking around them and no one offered help or even gave her a smile of support. She needed time to think but Lola's sobbing and her lack of understanding of anything Jackie said made it hard to calm her. Toby and Vicky stroked Lola's hair and told her over and over that it would all be all right but they didn't seem convinced and Jackie couldn't work out how to make what had happened seem normal in anyway.

But after a while Lola looked up from Jackie's lap and Toby and Vicky pointed out the chickens outside and the pictures of the things they could do at the hotel. Then Jackie managed to manoeuvre them all outside, where they found a table and chairs overlooking the grass sloping down to the sea. Up in the sky the large black hawks circled as usual and could be seen settling on the towers then launching themselves off over the sea wall. Whilst on the grass their distant cousins pecked around the trees, not managing more than a flutter every now and again up into the air. The children wandered around the lawns chasing the wild fowl and Jackie ordered some drinks from an attentive waiter who appeared smiling at her side. It was a beautiful setting, sitting in a white wicker chair, with a white wicker table, drinking freshly squeezed mango juice, watching the birds, the sea, the palm trees and the children. And Jackie felt herself understand the point of luxury. Being comfortable, being waited on, having calm and occupied children. Now she could think. And she decided she needed to talk to Andrew. Andrew was sensible. Andrew was rational and good at problem solving. He would know what to do. She told the children she was going to find a phone and headed back to the reception. Behind the counter was a little middle aged woman who must have seen the police come in but rather than judge or comment she managed to show her sympathy with a warmth and smile that Jackie needed. She gently touched Jackie's hand and pointed to a phone booth further down the hall. She then sorted out change for her and wrote down the code for England saying 'Yes speak to your husband. He will tell you what to do. But they will be back soon. They always are'. Jackie smiled back at her feeling reassured, trying not to let the words 'tell you' grate too much, and headed off to the phone.

'Andrew. It's me.' It felt strange hearing his voice again.

'Jackie. Lovely to hear from you. It's seemed like ages. Are you having fun?'

Jackie had wanted this first conversation to be full of how wonderful Cuba was, how interesting their trip had been and all about the sights, the people and the politics. But after a few half-hearted sentences trying to sound calm and positive she gave in and explained everything that had just happened. She told him about Olivia and Lola coming with them from Trinidad and described the doubts she had had about staying somewhere so luxurious and about the argument and then told him how the police had arrived out of nowhere and taken them away. Andrew in turn asked all the right questions and remained calm and un-phased as she knew he would. He asked whether the police had given any clues as to when they would be back, whether she had asked any of the locals if this was a common occurrence and whether there was a tourist service at the hotel that could help them.

'It's an International hotel, Jackie. There must be some service for tourists who have problems when they are abroad. I'd ask at reception and find them. Otherwise find a tourist centre in Havana – but I think it's best if you stay at the hotel if you can - to be there when they get back. As a last resort you could always go the police, but I would probably avoid this if you can. You don't want to make things worse.'

'Thanks Andrew. I really needed to speak to someone. That all makes a lot of sense. I knew you would be able to help me think it through. I think I've seen a sign for the tourist office in the foyer here.' She paused for a while feeling the anxiety sink lower and it was like being held by a caring parent. 'It would have been nice if you had come, you know. You would have liked it here. It's really interesting and we've seen so much of what feels like the real Cuba. No tourists anywhere, just Cuban families having their lives. The way we've always done holidays in the past, Andrew. I've thought about you, Andrew. Often.'

'That's nice Jackie. It's nice to know. I would have liked to have come too, but didn't really feel I could with the way things were.'

'Well. Let's talk when we get back. I'd better go now and try and get this all sorted out.'

'Yes. Go to the tourist office at the hotel. But I do think you were risking it, bringing that woman along with you. It's a Communist country. They are bound to be touchy about tourists talking to locals.'

'OK Andrew,' Jackie said, feeling a familiar wave of tension starting to build up.

'Bye then, darling,' he said. 'Do as I say and I'm sure you will be fine. But don't get into anymore trouble without me. OK. See. You do need me after all!'

Jackie put the phone down quickly.

Why was it, just as she allowed herself to warm to him, he did something that pressed so many buttons. A look, a tone of voice, a single word seemed to set off a chain reaction, linking the present to all other events in the past. It was as if her brain had a network of patterns all waiting to be lit up by something simple that could light up all the other 'something simples' that had happened before. And the sum of all those lights was so much greater when they all shone in full floodlit force together. Once, they had been snuggling in bed and she had even began to fancy him, when the subject of her much smaller, but well deserved, annual salary came up and he had kissed her on the forehead, saying: 'We could put that towards a new sofa', and she had felt a bit of her soul die. Another time she had taken his hand as they were walking through the park, but he squeezed it twice then pulled away and she felt like screaming at him. Such small things could have such devastating effects. But finding a tourist office was a good idea, as was staying at the hotel, so she headed back to the woman at the reception desk.

Carl emerged out of his room feeling battered and empty, to find Olivia waiting for him on a chair in the corridor. She looked drawn and tired and her eyes seemed less striking than when they had set off that morning, excitedly describing everything they were going to do in Havana, none of which had included being locked up in a police station and bullied by the police for many long hours. But she smiled, and her fading eyes still managed to shine as she wrapped her arms around him and they collapsed into each other. And Carl who had tried so hard to convince himself that everything would be fine felt himself well up in tears for the first time in years. The police showed them into the waiting car and they held hands and sat close as they were taken back to the hotel.

'Mama!' squealed Lola as they walked back into the hotel.

Lola threw her little body at her mother and buried herself into her stomach. They brushed noses, kissed each other's faces and reassured each other over and over again that everything was now back to normal and that they would never be separated again.

'I think,' said Jackie 'we all deserve a drink.'

'In fact,' she added 'I think we all deserve a couple of nights in a posh hotel. What do you think? Then you can tell us all about what happened.'

Olivia made a few half hearted attempts to disagree, but Carl placed his arms around both her and Jackie, and with the children clinging onto all their legs it was agreed that luxury was what they all needed and that most importantly they needed showers, drinks and some food cooked, served and cleared away by someone else.

Fourteen

The nice woman at reception was still on duty and booked them in, smiling at Jackie smiling. 'I'm glad it is now OK. You will have a lovely time here. It is our most wonderful hotel in the whole of Cuba.' They then picked up their bags and headed off to find the lift. As they turned out of the entrance hall, the floor turned from marble to thick carpet and they found the brass-fronted lift with its golden dial above showing the different floors. The doors soon opened and a hotel porter in a smart black uniform helped them in with their bags. It felt like a 1950s Hollywood film and no one would have been surprised if Jack Lemmon and Tony Curtis had followed them in, in their high heels and fur trimmed hats to the sound of some old time crooner. The walls were all mirrored and they grinned at each other's reflections as they let the tension of the past few hours let itself out in giggling and jokes.

Their rooms were off a deep purple corridor with rich carpet and they disappeared inside to freshen up for the evening. Jackie's room was smaller than she had expected with the two single beds tightly fitting into the space next to her own, but she was so relieved to have Carl and Olivia back that she flopped back on her bed and pulled her kids over to her and they lay, laughing, tickling each others' well known tickling spots and talking about how nice it would be to have anything they wanted that evening. Jackie had always had a wonderfully physical relationship with her children. When Toby had first been born she had held him close and watched, relieved, as he immediately calmed and settled. From that moment, she had felt that she could be a mother, and that her children would want her to look after them. Her children still came into her bed for their morning cuddle and throughout the day they would forever jump into her lap or wrap their arms around her middle, the connection allowing them to recharge and get on with the task of becoming independent. But all this contact had contributed to her growing distance from Andrew. She didn't need to be held at the end of the day, when she had already spent so much time sharing her body with her kids. And sometimes her bed felt like the only place she could get any space to make her boundaries intact again. And here on the bed, in Cuba, after a day of confusion and difficulty the simple pleasure of nuzzling took them all back to a place of comfort and calm.

'Right. Dinner,' Jackie said as they all met up outside the lift.

'Right. Drink,' said Carl.

And they got back in the lift, this time looking at each other in the mirrors with their clean and brushed hair and the poshest clothes they could find. Jackie had her red dress on, which had become the mark of a night out and Olivia looked stunning in a white top and skirt and some of Jackie's jewellery. Even Carl had washed and was wearing clean jeans and a tight white shirt which showed off his chest muscles underneath. His woolly hat was nowhere to be seen.

'We all look lovely,' said Vicky. 'Isn't this nice? Like one big family all together again.'

The restaurant was enormous with circular tables, white table cloths and people from everywhere other than Cuba having their night out. The waiters were smart in their dark blue uniforms and they were welcomed and waited on in a way that seemed genuine and happier than they seen in some of the more run-down places. They sat down and examined the extensive menu and ordered wine and more wine as the night progressed. The children behaved impeccably and chatted to each other, pointing out the other guests, while the adults drank away the problems of the day. Then the music started. A mass of black-tied men appeared at one end of the room and laid out their instruments and music stands and then the sound of Cuba came in force across the tables. Not like the bands they had seen in the street, or those that had played to them in the cafés who had seemed raw and natural, but a full- on force of rehearsals, professionalism and just pure volume. Each single guitar produced the sound of multiple guitars and the multiple guitars created a frenzy of finger work and chords. The drums beat out and the brass section introduced the power of that big band noise that would have excited any 1950s conductor. And then a woman appeared from the wings wearing a bold and bright costume that glittered in the lights as she sang and swung her hips to the music. The audience watched and applauded, drank their wine and applauded some more. There was none of the dancing that they had seen in the square in Trinidad or the bars of Havana but the air was rich with pleasure and the luxury of being entertained in style. And Jackie watched as Carl and Olivia became engrossed in each other and looked on as their hands touched under the table, their legs became entwined and they laughed at each other's jokes in the way only those in love can. It had been a while since Jackie had felt like that and she felt excited, envious, sad that intimacy had gone from her own life and a sense of scepticism that it would last; that strange mix of feelings all flooding in with the wine and the night. Wanting something again, remembering how wonderful it feels, yet a life-time's worth of evidence telling you that it fades into nothing. But not always. She always thought 'But not always'. Sometimes it must last. Some people love each other until the end. If you make the right choice you could find the right person. Not often. She didn't know anyone. But it does happen. It must happen. Not to her. Not in her marriage. But perhaps it could next time. There could always be the next time. Not now. Not with the kids. But perhaps in the future. She could be free to try again. And maybe she would make a better choice. A more lasting choice. And then it could be her wrapped around a man whose eyes she wanted to look into rather than avoid. And a man whose hands and mouth were the ultimate source of intimacy and interest.

The children began to fade and flounder and as they lounged upon each other, Jackie gathered them all up and said that it would be nice for them all to sleep with her for the night. No one complained as she manoeuvred them to the lift and as she looked back through the doors she could see Carl and Olivia finishing the dregs of their drinks and pulling each other up from the table.

....

'Jackie?' said Carl over breakfast.

'You're looking perky,' she said, smiling.

'I've asked Olivia to marry me. Come to England. Live with Me.'

'Blimey!' said Jackie. 'Quick work. What did she say?'

'Yes!' said Carl flushing. 'She said 'Yes'! God! Shit! I mean it's great! Blimey. I'm going to marry her!'

Fifteen

'Carl,' said Olivia as they loaded their bags into the car. 'Carl. We need to talk.'

'I know Olivia, and we have forever to talk now. I can tell you all about my life and I can find out all about yours. We can share our stories and then we can have new stories together. It's going to be wonderful.' He pulled her towards him and kissed her, brushing her hair back to see her face.

'Carl,' she said pushing him back. 'Carl. I can't marry you. I can't leave Cuba. My family. My history. My mother wouldn't cope without me. It's a wonderful country and I am part of it. I would be lost in England. I can't marry you.'

'But you said "Yes". What about everything we said last night? What about everything we did?'

'I should never have said it all. I have Lola. I have a mother. I wasn't thinking properly. Carl. I just can't. Let's not argue. I can't go with you and I need to get back home.'

The taxi took them to the train station in the centre of Havana, where they found hordes of people lining the platforms sitting on whatever was around to keep them off the floor. Mothers were trying to distract their children with stories, songs and games and those who had given up either had kids rolled up asleep on the floor or playing precariously close to the edge of the platform. There was a train to Trinidad in a couple of hours, which was amazingly soon for Cuban time, and Olivia seemed to think nothing of sitting down with the others to wait. She had tried to persuade Carl to go into Havana with Jackie and the kids but he had refused and now sat next to her in the shade of the platform roof, whilst Lola rested on her mum's knee and held his hand.

He watched the world around him. A world which now seemed full of families. All adults had children and all the women seemed to come in pairs. Some were with their mothers, friends or sisters but many were with men and all the families were busy, chaotic, frantic even, but engaged and involved in the world. Carl had always liked being his own boss, being able to sleep, eat and see friends whenever he felt like it. Now he thought of his calm, controlled and solo existence and felt alone. He squeezed Lola's hand and stroked her hair but Olivia avoided his eyes, choosing to stare at the pages of her unread book. He knew he could have been a good father to Lola and he knew that he would have loved Olivia. They would have been good for him and he would have tried so hard to make it all work.

Time passed and eventually as the sun was becoming too hot and the shaded platform no longer gave them any cover, the train arrived.

'Olivia' he asked. 'Are you sure? We would be good together.'

She looked at him at last and held his head in her hands.

'I know,' she said 'but I can't leave here. I am Cuban. I belong here.'

There was a pause, a silence, then the noise of the people piling onto the train broke into their thoughts and Carl helped her onto the train and carried Lola up the steps. He watched through the crowded window as they made their way to find a seat and saw them settle themselves amongst all the other families. They laid their books on their knees, got out their drinks, placed their bags under their seats. Then looked at him. Lola smiled and waved and Olivia stared, trying to burn his face onto her memory. And Carl just raised his hand as the tears flowed down his face and the train pulled away.

'She belongs here,' he thought. 'It's right,' he thought. 'Just a holiday romance,' he thought. 'I'll get over it,' he thought.

And he watched the back of the train head off into the distance leaving dust and quiet in its wake, thinking 'Now what? Now what do I do with the rest of my life?'

....

Ernesto welcomed Jackie and the children back into his house and they felt at home as they walked up his winding marble staircase and saw the familiar sight of hanging washing, large green shiny plants, the flimsy iron balcony and the plastic lobsters stuck onto the wall. He carried their bags into their rooms and the children flopped onto the large bed as Jackie pulled on the wooden revolving fans on the ceiling.

'I've never really liked hotels,' said Jackie. 'Much too posh. Could be anywhere in the world. This is much better.'

The three of them lay for a while, moving in and out of each other, so as to be held without getting too hot and Jackie stroked their backs in turn when they manoeuvred themselves to be next in line. They watched the fans cranking as they went round and stared at the wooden panelled walls and high shuttered windows. They could hear the TV from the next room blaring out some sporting event and listened to Ernesto and his wife as they chatted from one room to the next. It was nice here; just the three of them; being close. No tensions. No frustrations. No irritations.

'This is OK. I could do this. I am OK on my own. We would be fine,' Jackie thought. 'I could be a single parent.'

'Let's go to the Cathedral Square,' she said, sitting up. 'Let's have a drink and watch the world go by.'

'We could see the painters,' said Toby. 'Oscar might be there.'

'That's true. I didn't think of that,' she said, smiling. 'I'll just get washed then we can go.'

Sixteen

Jackie and the kids set off from Ernesto's ready for the midday sun in their hats and layers of sun cream. The streets were dusty and hot and the shade from the tall Colonial houses was too narrow to provide any real cover. They saw the same one-legged dog that had been there before, still hopefully wrapped up in a ball outside a kind woman's house. They saw the same elderly man lying in a doorway sleeping off the night before, still without his shoes and the barber was still standing on his crumbling step with his two fluorescent strips, cutting a young man's jet black hair as the electricity went on and off. And as they walked, people watched them from behind their glassless barred windows rocking in their chairs, drinking their juice as the white people suffered the heat. The local children sidled up to them in their bare feet and ragged clothes with their hands out, and thin adults with wrinkled rubbery skin asked for money for their children. The shelves in the chemist's shop were still half empty, and outside the bars men in white shirts stood touting for custom, but in a way that said they were happier not really waiting on anyone at all.

When they turned the corner the familiar square spread out ahead of them. The cathedral reflected the orange light of the sun and the glass was black against the stone. And the square was busy with Cuban life. Along the line of shade sat the Cuban men and women with their large cigars, Che Guevara T-shirts or brightly-coloured dresses available for photographs, and the fortune teller still sat in the corner, in her white dress at her white table, ready to read people their cards. The café was busy with tourists sitting under their umbrellas drinking cold beers, whilst the restaurant musicians played and sang and offered their hats around for money. They found themselves a table and sat down. Jackie pulled her hair up to try and cool her neck and the children blew on each other's faces although their breath wasn't much cooler than the air around them. Jackie glanced over to the wall where the painters sat, and could see Ralpho sitting on a step painting the Cathedral with a few finished pictures displayed beside him. But Oscar was nowhere to be seen. Then against the wall she saw the old man in his white shirt, tight belt and loose trousers swaying to the music.

'Look kids,' said Jackie. 'It's that dancing man again.'

He moved forward towards them, watching Jackie as his arm passed across his body, and he danced with his invisible lover to the sound of the band. His eyes closed and his flattened hand held onto his chest as his hips moved and his feet tapped out the beat. Jackie watched and felt the same sense of loss and love she had felt before. He seemed so stuck in the past but so calm and content. Then she felt a hand pressed on her shoulder and looked up to see Oscar leaning over her smiling.

'Hey!' he said. 'I wondered when I'd see you again. Can I join you?'

He sat down and the children chatted over each other telling him about their trip. They told him about the pigeons in the mountains, the storms and the rain and the lizard that liked to hang from ears. Then he heard all about the fishing and the sea in Trinidad and bobbing about in inflatables and about the posh hotel in Havana and their late night and all the food and music. And they told him all about meeting Olivia and Lola.

'Then Olivia decided to go home,' said Toby. 'Carl's taken her to the train station. I think they are in love.'

'I saw them kissing,' said Vicky, giggling.

'The police took them away,' said Toby. 'We didn't see them for ages. Lola was really upset.'

Oscar raised his eyebrows at Jackie and looked worried.

'Why don't you two go and have a chat with Ralpho,' said Jackie. 'And Oscar and I can catch up.'

The children took their drinks and soon Jackie could see them sitting on the steps chatting to the painters and colouring in their own versions of the square.

'It's nice to be back,' she said looking at Oscar properly now. 'You look well. Happy I mean.'

'I'm pleased to see you. I'm not used to missing someone,' he said. 'It was a surprise.'

He pulled his chair up close as she explained what had happened with the police, all the while struggling to recapture the anxiety of it, as his knees touched hers and his fingers brushed her legs, encouraging her to talk more. Jackie had often wondered whether there really was some sixth sense that enabled you to feel that you were being looked at, or in someone's thoughts. Sometimes it felt so clear that she could feel eyes burrowing into the back of her head or just know that someone was thinking about her. And now a sense of Oscar's passion seemed to emit from his every pore and seep into hers. But as she talked about the police and their incessant questioning Oscar smiled and nodded as if unaware that his body was calling her. He then explained that the regime didn't like tourists befriending locals and were worried that Cuba's reputation would be damaged overseas. He also described how if you were found criticising the government three times you could end up in prison and how they hated Cubans marrying foreigners and leaving the country but so far hadn't prevented it. And all the while, Jackie could feel a heat coming off his body that had very little to do with the sun and the time of the day.

'Jackie,' said Oscar 'Can we go out for dinner tonight?'

'That would be lovely. The kids would love to see the city at night again,' said Jackie.

'How about without the kids?' said Oscar. 'Just this once. You must be owed a night off. Carl could look after them.'

Jackie watched him for a while. His loose white shirt hinted at a body that needed to be touched and his eyes burrowed into hers. It had been a long time since she had wanted to be with someone like this. All those teenage years of passion, crushes, kissing and fantasising about the next boyfriend even before the current one had properly run his course. Yet she had grown into a woman who avoided touch. A woman for whom sex had become a part of routine at best, and duty at worst, and who could now understand why women who did it for money refused to kiss and could find solace in their own internal worlds of distraction. How did that happen? Where did all that passion go? How could a body once soft and spontaneous feel like it was constantly cloaked in impenetrable armour. And now, in front of Oscar the armour was on fire as her other, better and sexier self began to break through.

'It's true,' she said 'I've done my time. I deserve a night off. You can teach me to dance.'

'I'll teach you whatever you like,' said Oscar.

'And I'll teach you straight back,' she said, laughing, and took his hand which was now lounging on her thigh as if it belonged there.

Seventeen

Carl agreed to take on the children for the evening. His woolly hat was firmly back on his head and he had a haunted look that Jackie had never seen before. She tried to offer useless words of reassurance and made platitudes that were so obviously meaningless, that she let him withdraw into his own world. Now was the time for distance and space as the healing remedy, but any words to that effect were bland and pointless, so she just put her arm around his shoulder and handed him over to the care of her children who were pretty efficient at distracting anyone from anything. Then she showered, covered herself in a range of differently smelling products, which she then promptly washed away to avoid giving off the air of a department store's ground floor, put back on her favourite perfume, gave her red dress yet another airing, painted her toe nails and was finally ready, feeling relieved that going out wasn't always so stressful. She left the house to satisfying calls of 'Mummy you look amazing!', 'Mummy you're beautiful!' and 'You smell lovely', and then headed off to the Cathedral square to meet Oscar.

As she set off into the evening, the sun was still up, giving the sky a glow of reds and oranges, but within minutes it had gone and night had set in. But the city was far from ready to sleep and the bars were filling up and the bands were tuning their instruments for the evening ahead. Jackie found Oscar sitting on the kerb in the square looking washed and groomed for their date and they kissed each other on the cheek as usual, but this time it was brushed with a newer taste of possibility.

'I want to show you the Malecón,' said Oscar. 'Everyone must walk along the Malecón. It is where Cubans are most alive.'

'I'm in your hands,' said Jackie and he put his arm around her shoulder and she felt the first layer of her armour shed itself and be trampled under their feet.

They headed down to the seafront and found Cubans meeting Cubans along the vast wall that stretched in front of the rocks and wound into the distance of the city edge. The sky was black but a slight white light hinted at the horizon as it joined the deserted sea. The warm breeze made them walk close into each other and Oscar pointed out memories for her to take home. There were groups of young men jumping off the rocks and squealing as they hit the dark water and young couples sitting on the wall watching all the other young couples walk past. There were elderly women wheeling prams full of small cones of home roasted peanuts for sale and men driving vans selling cans of beer or bottles of something they had brewed in their kitchens. There were men playing guitars, as their friends sang and beat time on the wall, and young women walking arm in arm looking at the men.

Jackie and Oscar sat on the wall to watch the night and curled into each other against the cooling air. On the other side of the road was a never ending line of colonial buildings overlooking the sea. At one time this must have been the home to the richest playboys of Cuba with easy access to the casinos, piano bars and local women who had resorted to making the most of the American presence in their city. But now piles of rubble lay at the foot of the walls and many were just skeleton blocks of their former selves. Then suddenly out of nowhere was a massive explosion. Jackie jumped and would have been more frightened had anyone else reacted but the noise was generally ignored and people just carried on doing whatever they were doing.

'Wow!' said Jackie 'What was that?'

'It's the cannon,' said Oscar 'to mark the landing of Castro and his men. It goes off every night. I'm so used to it I forgot to warn you!'

'Oscar,' said Jackie 'What's it like living here? I've been here nearly two weeks and I've got such mixed feelings.'

'That's because it's mixed. It's good and bad,' he said 'like everywhere I guess. Right now, I want to show you the best. Let's dance.'

He helped her down from the wall and led her away from the Havana she knew and through a maze of narrow roads and ruined buildings to where the music got louder and the streets got busier. This was the city that she had read about in the guide books where you went when you travelled without children. The city of late nights, rum, sexy dancing, single men on the prowl and single women who could handle endless attention from men attracted by foreign looks and the possibility of marriage and a passport. Oscar held her hand and led her up to the door where people were spilling out onto the street. There were men in white T-shirts, tight trousers and smart pointy leather shoes milling everywhere and women in short skirts and high heels lounging against the walls watching the new arrivals. A large bouncer let them in through the door and Oscar quickly paid and steered her upstairs where a wall of lights and noise hit them as they entered an enormous room full of bodies, sweat and energy.

'I need a drink,' said Jackie, remembering that it had been a long time since she had been to a club like this. 'I think I need to be a bit drunk.'

'A bit drunk maybe. But not much,' said Oscar. 'The music will make you high enough and you need to think. At least at first.'

He bought her a rum and coke which evaporated as soon as she put it to her lips and he swiped the glass off her and led her into the mass of dancing bodies.

'You follow me,' he said 'and you'll be fine. Let your hips move and feel the beat in your chest. And feel sexy!' He laughed with shining eyes and she felt that she might at least manage that last part of the deal.

Oscar held her hands and they stepped from side to side in the way she had done back home in her thwarted salsa classes. But this time she was with a man, whose arms were strong and had a command, and made her happy to be under his control. He put his hand on her waist and pulled her closer and they continued to step as she felt his arm move through his shirt. Within minutes he spun her round, then spun her back and they began to move together with their steps in reflection and her hips offering a mirror to his. There were spins, and swaying, and hands which sent her any which way he wanted her to go and when they worked together like a beautiful system she glowed and when she got it wrong she threw her head back and laughed as Oscar brought them back to the rhythm of the moves. Sometimes the music was so fast it was hard to catch the beat and her feet seemed hardly to skim the floor as she found herself just moving rather than counting out the time, whilst Oscar did his own spins and steps and moved his hips in a way that she didn't know men could. Then at times the music slowed and became smooth and luxurious and they moved closer into each other and she felt contained and calm for a while.

'You can dance,' said Oscar as they left the dance floor for a drink. 'You are wonderful to lead. You move well.'

'That was amazing,' Jackie said 'What a wonderful thing to be able to do. It's so hard at first but then it's kind of animal. So raw. If I didn't have to concentrate so hard most of the time it would almost be natural. You're a good teacher.'

'I know,' said Oscar laughing. 'I'd love to be able to teach more.'

'But can't you?' said Jackie.

'But only here,' said Oscar. 'Only in Cuba. I'd love to travel and teach. Teach people to dance who think they can't. Come to England. Teach people like you. In Italy. Spain. China, even. All the places I'll never see.'

'Oscar,' said Jackie, putting her arms around the back of his neck. 'Now will you tell me what it's like to live here? Really like. To be Cuban. To grow up here. And to have to stay here.'

Oscar brushed her hair back from her face and looked at her. Her eyes were bright from the dancing but looked serious and determined and her skin was flushed and wet. He touched her mouth with his finger then leant forward and kissed her. And Jackie didn't flinch, or cough or move away but felt herself pulling him into her and the final part of her armour vanished from her body into the heat of the dancing room. They looked up into each other and kissed again, this time with more urgency and passion.

'Let's go back to my flat,' said Oscar. And Jackie took his hand and firmly led him out of the club and back towards the seafront.

By now the Malećon was thriving with people pouring in or out of the clubs or just out to watch the night. The sky and sea were merged in their blackness but the wall was lit by occasional bars along the street. They bought some beers from a passing man and drank as they walked, this time with more purpose and direction than before. And every now and again they would stop to kiss, and giggled amongst the other lovers stopping to kiss by the sea wall. And as they walked, Oscar told her of his dreams and his frustrations with a country that had so much soul and spirit but was also a prison. He described how he loved the city with its history and culture but couldn't bear that that was all he knew. He had read of other countries with their music, art, buildings and countryside, yet had only ever seen Cuba. He loved what Castro had done and was so proud to be part of a country that had stood up to the US, yet hated that they had no choice over what job they did or where they lived.

'The country needs investment. And we can't have it,' he said. 'We have great education but can't use it after we are qualified. We have a great health care system but no drugs when we get to hospital. And we have all this land for farming but only hoes and cattle to farm it with. Sometimes I could scream. I feel so trapped. All these tourists come into our country, take their photos and are wowed by the old cars and the crumbling buildings. Then they leave. They fly out. We see the planes. We know where the airport is but we are always left behind. Behind, for the next lot of tourists to watch and be amazed by. It's like being in a living museum.'

He talked with an anger that was contagious and Jackie could feel herself feeling his frustration as if it were her own and held him closer and kissed him with more passion at each break in their walk.

At last they reached his iron door and they walked their way up the winding marble staircase to find his small flat at the top. He had a balcony like Ernesto's that looked down into his neighbour's courtyard below and he led her into his room where the fans were on and the large oak bed was impossible to ignore.

'I feel strange,' said Jackie 'I haven't done this with anyone other than Andrew for such a long time.'

'Are you having doubts?' asked Oscar, pulling her towards him and placing his hands around the back of her neck.

She placed a hand on his chest and could feel his heart pounding, willing her on. She undid his shirt and pulled it off and ran her fingers down his dark wet body.

'I guess that's a "No" then,' said Oscar laughing, and he carelessly undid the zip down her back and let her red dress finally fall at her feet in the way it had been designed to do.

'It's a "No",' she laughed, and they kissed and rolled onto the bed.

At first Jackie wanted to be under the sheet and found herself asking what he liked and what he wanted her to do. But as they explored and twisted and wrapped each other up, her mind went silent and she entered that place of passion and intimacy, where time is lost. A place where bodies know where to touch, and with what, and for how long, and a place where every place becomes exciting and alive. A place of peace and the moments she had so longed for. She found herself doing things she hadn't done for years and responding in ways she thought she was beyond. Her body was alert to his every touch and she loved being able to turn him on and listen to his noises that she claimed as hers. And in the pauses between, they laughed like teenagers and talked about who the other had enabled them to become. She had so longed for intimacy and had found it with someone she hardly knew, yet could feel so close to, as the lack of knowing gave her the freedom to be best version of herself.

The hours carelessly rolled by until the birds started to sing and the morning light made its way through the drawn curtains.

'I need some sleep,' said Jackie, rolling over.

'You sleep then,' said Oscar and he rolled up behind her and their bodies fitted together like spoons as he kissed the back of her neck. 'Thank you for a wonderful night.' But Jackie was already asleep.

Eighteen

Jackie awoke to find Oscar still curled up around her. She unravelled his arms, kissing his fingers as she lifted them off her shoulders, and slipped quietly into her clothes. She left him a note and went back to find her kids happily having breakfast with Carl in Ernesto's kitchen. There was the usual huge jug of fresh mango juice on the table and Ernesto's wife quickly made her an omelette and brought her a plate of various fruits, all of which she devoured within minutes.

'Mummy you are starving,' said Vicky.

'You've eaten it even faster than me,' said Toby.

'Must be all that dancing,' laughed Carl, although his eyes didn't quite light up the way they usually did when he teased her.

Jackie laughed along and told them of her walk along the Malecón and how Oscar had taught her to salsa and although she felt a wave of guilt and thought briefly of their father, the children seemed easy with her story of sleeping on Oscar's sofa and surprisingly happy, given that she had left them alone for an evening. She had always felt the need to put them to bed. But here they were, in Cuba, playing with local children, catching pigeons, wandering off to fish, very often out of her sight and they seemed more settled, relaxed, taller even than all her input at home had managed.

Today was market day and the children wanted to spend their holiday money on souvenirs, so after they had lathered themselves with sun tan cream, they all set off to the Cathedral Square. Carl wore his woolly hat, even though it was warming up to be another roasting day, and he walked several paces behind the rest of them with his head lowered, unaware as they walked past their daily dose of the one-legged pink dog and the barber with his flashing fluorescent strip. As they approached the square Jackie's flashbacks of legs and wet bodies became stronger and she struggled to chat mindlessly to her kids as the waves of smells and tastes and images blocked her mind. And as they turned the corner and she saw Oscar sitting on the curb, her body gave her a living memory of what it had felt the night before. They sat down with him and Carl went to buy their drinks from the cafe.

'How are you this lovely morning?' Oscar said taking her hand.

'My light is on. In fact all of me is still on,' she said. 'I like feeling like this. It's wonderful.'

'Is he OK?' asked Oscar, nodding over to Carl.

'No,' said Jackie. 'He hardly speaks and he is just so sad. His light has gone out.'

Carl came back and joined them, managing to hand out the drinks without looking at anyone. The kids wandered off to see the artists and he sat down, quietly looking at the ground. All chat suddenly seemed wrong and they sat in silence, subdued by Carl's mood. And in front of them the square continued with its rituals as the men and women smoked their huge Havana cigars for the tourists, the woman in white waited to tell fortunes, the band played and even the old man could be seen with his arms crossing his chest swaying in time to the salsa beat.

'This is where I paint, Jackie,' said Oscar. 'Every day I paint and every day I see this. The tourists love it. They take their photos and are wowed by our culture and our music. And then they leave. But this never changes. It is always the same. My life is always the same.'

And at that moment the troop of men and women in brightly coloured costumes walking on stilts entered the square playing their instruments and collecting money from the crowds that gathered around surprised by the novelty of what they saw.

'It's like Ground Hog Day,' said Jackie.

'What's that?' said Oscar

'A film,' said Jackie 'About a man who gets stuck in the same day over and over again.'

'A film I've never seen,' said Oscar.

They collected up the children and wandered to the market place which lay just outside the cathedral square. The pavements were strewn with women offering to plait Jackie's or Vicky's hair and photos of previous plaitings were constantly pushed under their noses. There were small cars surrounded by a large yellow sweet corn shell and their drivers hassled them for the chance to drive them somewhere they didn't want to go. And there were horse and carts waiting in case they might change their mind and take a trip somewhere.

They entered the market, which was a vast series of awnings covering row after row of tables, with their owners proudly showing off their wares. There were stalls of jewellery with necklaces and bracelets made out of red, brown and black seeds from melons, apricots and mangoes. Even sweet corn had been dyed red and threaded to be worn in layers. There were mechanical tortoises made out of coconut shells, miniature airplanes made out of old tins of fizzy drink and fantastic sculptures made of wood. There were the usual paintings of Che Guevara, and every now and again a man would mutter 'CDs, buy your CDs' under his breath just loud enough to hear, and would look at them hoping to sell them his home made copies of non-Cuban music. It all looked so creative, so original, and so different. The Cubans could make something out of nothing, to turn other people's rubbish into their art and nothing was ever seen as just waste. Then when they turned the corner to start the next lane of buzzing stalls they found the same necklaces, tortoises, sculptures and airplanes and a different man muttering about his illegal goods. The sun was by now high in the sky and the market trapped in the heat, and although the kids were loving choosing what to buy for themselves and their friends Jackie began to find the market overwhelming and oppressive.

'I need to get of here,' she said. 'I'm hot and it's all just more of the same. Where do they get this all from? I thought they had made it but they can't have all made the same stuff. And it's all the same price. I don't get it. I need to get some air. I'm beginning to feel a bit ill.'

The children quickly spent their money and although they complained and moaned they were also relieved to get out of the heat. They found Oscar and Carl sitting in silence out on the curb and decided to take a trip in a horse and cart to get some air and cool off. The kids sat up front with the driver, leaving the adults to sit in an uncomfortable silence in the back. Jackie wanted to snuggle up close to Oscar but felt she

167

couldn't; Oscar wanted to plan another night out with Jackie but that seemed inappropriate; and Carl just sat, eyes fixed on nothing, saying nothing, hearing nothing but preventing anything else from being said or done. But at least the air was cooler as they rode along and the children were entertained by the horse and a driver who was happy to point out child-friendly parts of the city. So the kids saw the park and other horse and carts whilst Jackie and Oscar absorbed the heat from each other's bodies and touched fingers in the back.

'Carl,' said Oscar eventually, as the silence became too much 'why don't you go and see Olivia. You could get the train down or I could help you get a lift.'

Carl slowly looked up and just shook his head.

'You have a couple more days until your flight. At least you could say goodbye properly.'

'No,' said Carl. 'There's no point. She has her life and I have to go back to mine. I have nothing to offer her.'

'She did love you, you know,' said Jackie. 'Anyone could see that.'

'But not enough,' said Carl.

'Leaving your country is a big thing,' said Jackie. 'Particularly when you have kids. I couldn't do it.'

'I could,' said Oscar.

'So could I,' said Carl.

'At least you can,' said Oscar.

'God, you're bitter,' said Carl.

'And you are just feeling so sorry for yourself,' said Oscar.

'Actually I'm sad. Really sad. Suddenly my life made sense. Now it doesn't. And I'm not sure what to do with it all now,' said Carl.

'I'm so sorry, Carl. It must be really hard. But we're on holiday. It's supposed to be fun,' said Jackie.

'Don't know why you're pretending you're so happy,' said Carl, snapping at her. 'You're as stuck as the rest of us.'

'Yes, but I'm here and I'm currently pretending I'm not stuck, so leave me out of it,' said Jackie.

'Ah, leaving, there's an interesting idea,' said Carl.

'Carl, stop it,' said Jackie. 'Don't take your problems out on me. I'll make my own decisions and you can make yours. You've no idea about my life. You're free to do whatever you want. I'm not. And nor is Oscar. So leave it out.'

Jackie and Oscar's fingers tightened in the private space on the seat between them in a bond against everything that was difficult in life. And quiet descended on the back of the cart as they spent the rest of the trip staring out in silence, working out whether their lot in life was worse or better than that of the others.

Nineteen

Then, it was their last night in Cuba. Although Jackie was tempted to take up Carl's offer to have the kids again for the evening she felt that they should all spend the night together and leave the holiday on a high. Oscar agreed to join them and first stop was a walk along the Malecón. Toby and Vicky were excited about having a late night and wandered along the sea wall watching the musicians, couples kissing and boys jumping into the sea.

'Hey kids, stand still a moment,' called Jackie.

And the huge bang of the cannon went off on time, making the kids, but no one else, squeal.

'I'm getting the hang of Havana,' she laughed.

'Welcome to my world,' said Oscar.

'I'd like your world,' said Carl. 'Stop moaning.'

'Don't start that again!' said Jackie.

'Mummy,' said Vicky 'why doesn't Oscar come to England with us. He could have our spare room.'

'He's not allowed darling. Remember I explained that people in Cuba don't have passports.'

'He could have mine,' said Carl.

They all laughed. Then laughed some more when they realised that Carl wasn't laughing. He was quietly looking at Oscar.

'You're my height, brown eyes, a bit older but you're doing alright for your age. And black. Those white passport guys can't tell one black guy from another. They'll never notice. Here, you can even have my hat.'

He placed his beloved woolly hat on Oscar's head and pulled it over his ears.

'Don't be mad,' said Jackie. But they all starred at Oscar then back at Carl.

'I've done a lot of thinking. I want to go and find Olivia and see if I can make something of my life with her. Help her and Lola. I could get a job, help them out. It would be better than going back to nothing,' said Carl, speaking quickly as if the stopper had been pulled out of the bottle.

'But your friends, your work, a career, your Mum?' said Jackie.

'I've thought a lot about my mum,' said Carl. 'She'd want me to do the right thing. Staying here is the right thing.'

'Oscar?' said Carl 'How about it?'

They found a restaurant and spent the evening planning, worrying, panicking, deciding it was a mad idea and then planning again. Their flight was booked for the following afternoon, which gave Oscar just under a day to decide what to take with him and for Carl to change his mind. But the more they talked the more convinced Carl was that this was the right future for him. And the more excited Oscar became. Carl described Olivia and his future with her, in increasingly glowing ways, whilst Oscar expanded on where he would go, what he could see and who he could become. And the children watched from one to the other, caught up in the excitement of the moment and the risk of the plot.

They finished their meal without noticing anything about what they had eaten or the band that was playing and walked their way back though the city. Oscar went off home and Jackie took Carl's arm as they walked up the hill to Ernesto's.

'You know, Carl,' she said gently 'you won't be able to leave if you give Oscar your passport. You'll be here for the innings. You could just stay and see how it works out with Olivia.'

'I know,' said Carl. 'But I need to work here and I can work as Oscar. And anyway he's moaned so much about being trapped it will shut him up for a while. And make him happy.'

'You're a good man Carl,' said Jackie. 'I shall miss you.'

And they made their way up Ernesto's winding staircase for the last time and went to bed.

In the morning Jackie packed up their things and they had breakfast as usual with Ernesto and his wife waiting on them for the last time. The kids buzzed with a renewed excitement and Carl's light was definitely back on as he wolfed down his food and laughed and chatted with the kids. They said their goodbyes and headed off to find Oscar, who took them inside, where everything was packed, ordered and ready to go. Everyone had slept on it and everyone had woken up more convinced than ever that it was the right thing to do.

Then Carl and Oscar quickly swapped their lives. They exchanged clothes, shoes, sunglasses, even washing things and towels. They filled each other's rucksacks and bags with all they could take and Jackie trimmed Oscar's hair to take a few years off. Then Carl gave Oscar his passport and placed his woolly hat upon his head and it was done. It was strange. They looked no different really but Oscar in his baggy low slung jeans, tight belt and T-shirt now had a South London feel to him and Carl in his loose white shirt and long shorts definitely looked more Cuban than English.

'This might actually work, you know,' said Jackie.

'You mean you weren't sure?' laughed Oscar. 'It'd better, or I'll end up in prison.'

'We all could,' said Carl.

'Could we, mummy?' asked Vicky.

'We'll be fine, darling. We've just got to get Oscar on and off the plane.'

'And not call him Oscar', said Toby.

'From now on I will call you Carl, Oscar,' said Vicky.

'Just Carl will be enough,' laughed Oscar. But it was beginning to feel serious.

They gathered up their belongings and left the flat feeling more subdued than before. Carl kissed them all goodbye and thanked Jackie for the envelope of cash she had given him. Then he walked off to the station and they were alone. And as they made their way back to the car the world seemed full of policemen. There were policemen hanging out on the corner of the street, policemen coming out of shops and policemen sitting in bars. All in their green uniforms, with their guns at their hips, looking for people who were breaking the law. People like them, which made looking innocent strangely hard.

Jackie took the children by the hand and tried to chat to them casually about their holiday and how great it had been, and the new Carl walked behind them with his rucksack on his back trying to look as if leaving Cuba was what he did on a regular basis. But their steps felt slow and their conversation was stilted and unreal and every now and again someone would over-laugh at something that was not that funny, then stop themselves and go silent. And the children resorted to not calling Oscar anything to avoid having to call him Carl, so he became 'you' or 'he' and Vicky even called him 'the hat man' which was funny but meant that they couldn't laugh at all.

Then eventually, and undetected, they reached the car, loaded up Oscar's bags and headed off to the airport. Jackie had by now become adept at missing the pot holes and Oscar's directions made the unsigned, unmarked roads much easier to navigate. And they began to relax.

The sights of Cuba were now familiar to Jackie and the kids and their trip to the airport felt like a summarised version of everything they had seen since they arrived. But Oscar stored all the sights and sounds to memory and made himself properly see what he had spent his life half-seeing. Old 1950's cars and cattle trucks passed them brimming with people. They saw hordes of hitchhikers under the bridges hoping for a lift and old men stood by the side of the road selling onions and garlic. There were paintings of Che Guevara on bill boards and the sides of buildings and the huge black hawks could be seen circling the tops of the buildings and soaring off into the distance.

'I'm getting out,' said Oscar quietly. 'My God, I'm going to do it.'

Leaving the car with the hire company was easy, but as they entered the airport the police reappeared, looking and watching for exactly what they were about to do. Oscar placed Carl's ear pieces into his ears, turned on his music and adopted the look of a bored 25 year old ready to go home. Then Jackie handed over their luggage and answered all the usual questions whilst Oscar stood back with the children who chatted away about anything they could think of. Then, they had their passports checked for the first time. And that was it. The first stage of the escape plan had happened without a hitch. The woman at the counter had simply smiled at them all, checked in their luggage and handed over their boarding passes. No extra questions, no suspicious looks and no alarm bells pressed under the bench. They walked off; not laughing or jumping or collapsing in a heap on the floor just walking as four normal people would do who were now ready to board their plane.

But the next stage was passport control. They stood in the queue behind the yellow line watching the passports being checked, photos being scrutinised and one by one, passengers looked up at the camera to have their faces recorded on the computer. Some custom controllers smiled, some were straight faced, some asked questions, some seemed bored and offhand. All were white and all had the power to ruin their plans and arrest Oscar. Jackie held the kids' hands and pointed out the cameras, the line, anything just to keep talking. And Oscar stood next to them smiling and somehow managing to look cool and calm. Jackie went up first with the kids. The woman smiled, asked them if they had enjoyed Cuba then leafed through each of their passports. Jackie lifted the kids up above the counter to have their photos taken, had hers done, adopting the neutral look of someone who would never dream of doing anything against the law, then they were through. They glanced back to see Oscar making his way up the desk.

'Did you have a nice holiday in Cuba?' he was asked.

'Yes great,' he said in his best London voice, handing over his passport open at the photo.

She looked down at it then back up at Oscar. She flicked through the rest of the passport then looked back at the photo.

'Where did you stay?' she asked.

'Oh everywhere' said Oscar keeping eye contact. 'We stayed with lots of families. It was great'.

She signalled for him to look up to the camera. The photo was taken and she handed back his passport. Carl's passport. Then he walked out the other side. There were no sirens blaring, no policemen pinning him to the ground. Just Jackie and the kids, to take his hands and head towards the loading bay.

Twenty

It was a long flight and although the kids spent some of the time watching films they were tired and irritable. Toby didn't like the kids' cartoons but wasn't allowed to watch anything more grown up and Vicky refused to eat the mash of chicken and vegetables, but was starving. They wriggled, moaned, fidgeted and resorted to poking and kicking each other to pass the time. Jackie went through her repertoire of distraction, negotiating, explaining, bribing followed by threatening then back to distraction, what she called 'the carrot stick carrot stick' approach, but just when one settled down the other found something new to be cross about. It was like having weather vanes for children who alternated in coming in and out of their bad behaviour houses. Then it was time to sleep and as they struggled to get comfortable, trying out every possible position feasible to two small children sitting in economy class, Jackie could see them both spiralling into that place of being too tired to do anything but sleep, but so over-tired that sleep is the last thing to happen. They would lie still for a while then twitch themselves awake just as the other was drifting off and the whole process of calming and stroking would have to start again. Oscar tried to help but soon got bored and put in head phones, closing his eyes to shut himself off from the noise that is family life. And for the first time in ages Jackie thought of Andrew. He may not have got involved spontaneously, and she may have had to tell him to put his newspaper down and help with the kids but at least they were his kids and he would always have helped out once asked. And he would have been someone else to distract them and someone else to call on for support even if she never did.

But at last the children fell asleep, lounging all over her in a way that left Jackie no place to rest other than just closing her eyes. And soon she too drifted off to re-live and re-feel the past two weeks. The plane landed and they seamlessly left the plane, passed through customs undetected, collected their bags and headed down to collect the tube into London.

Oscar was like a small child as the kids pointed out everything that was new and different and laughed at him feeling cold, putting on Carl's hat and doing up his jacket. And as Carl walked into the slave plantation to find Olivia sitting back outside the toilet selling toilet paper, they arrived at Waterloo station to meet Andrew down by the river. And as Olivia leapt up and flung her arms around his neck even more wildly than she had in his fantasies, Jackie and Oscar said goodbye at the top of the steps.

'It's been lovely knowing you,' she said. 'Thank you for making me feel good again.'

'I was lucky to meet you. You are a wonderful woman,' said Oscar. And they held each other just too long in a way that the children wouldn't notice.

He hugged the kids, then hugged Jackie again and set off across the bridge.

Then they walked down the steps to find Andrew. Toby and Vicky ran across to him, flinging their arms around him, climbing up his legs whilst Jackie loitered by the river for a while. Straight ahead was the long avenue with its musicians, street performers and voices from a hundred different countries; large concrete buildings with their cafes spilling out into the evening and the noise of a city ending its day in chat and drink. But over the railings was the water, the light, the bridge and peace. And the greens, blues and yellows which had been the setting of lovers captured so perfectly by artists years before. And there was Oscar disappearing into the distance. But those artists hadn't felt Oscar's arms around them and the fingers touching fingers. They hadn't known the breathing she had felt on her neck, the wet bodies, the entangled thighs and the moment when time is lost. And how easy it had felt and how much she had liked that best version of herself.

But that was then. And now was now. And now wasn't about any of that. It wasn't about arms or fingers or necks or breath. Now was about children telling their father all about their holiday. It was about ice creams, chasing pigeons and watching the seagulls. It was about tired children using up the last of their energy and about managing the switch from excitement to upset that could come out of nowhere. And mostly it was about trying to want to hold the hand of someone who would never know who she could be. Someone who never would or never could.

Jackie walked over to the railings and looked out. She felt the peace. It was still there and always would be. Then she turned away, walked back into the hustle of the day and kissed her children. And as Andrew picked up Vicky, she took his hand in hers and they went off to find some lunch.

THE END

Historical sources

I am not a historian and don't aspire to be but the following helped in writing this book.

Ernesto Guevara Lynch (2007). **The Young Che. Memories of Che Guevara**. Vintage Books: London.

Hugh Thomas. (1971). **Cuba. The pursuit of freedom**. Harper and Row: New York.

Fidel Castro (2008). **My Life**. Penguin Books: London.

1613472R0

Printed in Great Britain
by Amazon.co.uk, Ltd.,
Marston Gate.